A CHILL WIND

Ralston Store Publishing
P.O. Box 1684
Prescott, Arizona 86302

ISBN 978-1-938322-22-8

Professionally and lovingly edited by:
Jennifer Hope
www.MesaVerdeMediaServices.com

Front Cover Photograph by Kathleen Tyler Conklin.

Printed in the USA.

A CHILL WIND

Erica Einhorn

CHAPTER ONE

RED BLUFF WAS a pleasant enough place to live with fifteen thousand other people, most of whom didn't know what they were missing. They didn't know about the old days when there were more horses than people, when every house had a horse, and every horse had a pasture. Except back then, most of the houses were ranches, and there was more than one horse in the pasture. What was saddest, though, Jenna thought, was driving down some street that used to be rural and seeing white fences—some kept up, some with peeling paint—enclosing a whole pasture full of rich, succulent grass just longing to be munched on by a cow or a horse, but currently empty.

As sad as it made her, Jenna reminded herself how lucky she was to live on one of the remaining ranches. She continued brushing the black horse, one hand holding the brush, the other hand stroking the animal's soft coat. Not everyone brushed a horse this way, but it was something that her father had showed her. He said you need to give to the horse so the horse can give back to you. She could hear his voice even now, "Treat the horse

1

as you would like to be treated. No reason the golden rule can't apply to horses!" he'd say with a laugh. "Respect the horse, and he will respect you. Yes, you can get away with a brush in both hands and get the job done quicker. But if you were a horse, wouldn't you feel better with a loving hand stroking you as the dirt gets brushed away?"

She'd always followed this rule. No, it wasn't a rule. Her father didn't make rules, he only made suggestions. And she always followed them. Well, almost always. Jenna continued brushing and stroking the black coat. Early spring, it would be easier to use two brushes and get rid of some of the hair that was beginning to fall out with the coming warmth. But, truth of it was, she enjoyed stroking the horse as much as he enjoyed being stroked.

Magic nickered and turned his head to look at her. Jenna pulled his head closer and kissed his nose, and then kissed the white star on his forehead. She loved this horse. She was so grateful that he had survived the fire, though that thought made her feel guilty. After brushing his girth line, she moved to his other side to resume the brushing and stroking. When she finished, she stepped out of the stall to retrieve his hackamore from the tack room. Jet, her faithful Australian Shepherd, waited patiently outside Magic's stall. Jenna petted Jet's head and decided to ride bareback today. She normally rode saddled so she could bring her rifle with her to practice. Jenna was one of the top shooters in her mounted shooting group, and she intended to keep it that way. But, today, she'd leave the rifle and the saddle behind.

Slipping the hackamore over his nose and ears, Jenna led Magic out of the barn and into the paddock through the swinging door in his stall. Jenna had all the stalls in her new barn designed this way. A swinging door so the horse could exit or enter at will, and not get trapped inside—in case of fire. And an open gate led from the paddock into the big pasture where she kept her small herd of Angus cattle.

Magic followed her into the paddock like a docile little puppy. Once outside, a chill wind made Jenna shiver. She looked at the sky. Some clouds were approaching from the west, but they were still far enough away that she should be able to ride for an hour before any moisture hit.

"Magic, stay right here. I'll be right back." Jenna raced into the house to retrieve her jacket and came right back out. Jet followed her in and out of the house, but Magic hadn't moved at all and stood expectantly. She loved training him to verbal commands and loved teaching him tricks. Her favorite, however, was what she taught him after she sprained her ankle.

She swung up onto Magic's back, and they headed toward the back gate. Her property backed to a complex series of backcountry trails. Magic moved in close to the gate so Jenna could open it. They walked through, and Magic moved to the gate again. Jenna locked the gate, breathed deeply, looked up at the sky, and smiled.

Living in a rural environment like this gave Jenna great pleasure. It almost had her feeling like she lived a hundred years ago in a simpler time: a time of no car horns, traffic, or cell phones. She craved that but thought maybe what she really wanted to escape were the memories of death, fire, and betrayal.

When she felt the wind blow again, she buttoned her jacket against the chill. So much for early spring weather,

3

she thought. When they arrived at the fork in the trail, Jenna guided Magic to the right thinking that she needed something different today. The left was familiar and comfortable, but today she was up for some adventure— as long as it happened within the hour. She expected Sarah, her best friend, to come over after work.

Magic continued down the trail, with Jet a comfortable distance to the side. Jenna breathed deeply and tried to relax. These days, the only time she allowed herself to relax was when she was on her horse. She knew she needed to move on from Daniel's betrayal and the rest of that horrible year. But she didn't know how. Breathing deeply, she concentrated on the blue sky, now filling with clouds. Snow spit from above, and she tilted her cowboy hat to try to keep it out of her face. They wouldn't go much farther. Although she'd been on this trail many times before, it had been awhile. Was that a cow pie up ahead? She'd have to check her cattle when she got home.

Suddenly, it felt like someone had pulled a switch. The wind picked up, and the snow came down so heavy that Jenna couldn't see ten feet in front of her. They were too far from home to turn around in this; they needed to find shelter. Although she couldn't see her, Jenna heard Jet bark. "Come on, girl, I'll take care of you. Up!" She held out her foot, and Jet used it to boost herself into Jenna's lap. She unbuttoned her coat, pulled the dog closer, and wrapped the coat around her. Dropping the reins onto Magic's neck, she said, "Magic, see if you can find us some shelter." It wasn't something she had taught him, but sometimes it was like he understood her.

He turned onto a trail that Jenna couldn't see and started a steady uphill climb. The trees thinned out, and

Jenna hoped there was someplace they could get out of the heavy snow. With any luck, this would be one of those hard and heavy storms that blew through quickly. Judging by the bite of the chill wind, it might. She hoped that it wouldn't last long. If it did, they'd be in trouble. Unfortunately, she had her light spring jacket on and didn't even have a saddle blanket to crawl under. A black thought crossed her mind. They could freeze to death out here. Could anything else go wrong? No! In a situation like this, she needed to practice positive thinking, or they would not survive. Could anything go right? There, that made her feel better already.

CHAPTER TWO

SHERIFF JOSIAH STONE was on a mission. Well, actually, he was returning from his most recent mission which was appearing in federal court, a five-day ride from his home in Red Bluff. And now he was on the last day of the five-day return ride. But his task now was to get home and find out how much of a mess his town was in after his almost two-week absence.

Josiah hated that he had to leave *his* town in the hands of that no-account, incompetent, so-called deputy, Rawlins, but he didn't have a choice. No one else had stepped up. He would have loved to make Samuel the deputy. Unfortunately he had promised Eliza—she and Samuel ran the hotel in town—that he wouldn't. Everybody would be in better hands with Samuel. But he couldn't go against Eliza's wishes. The hardest part about that was that he couldn't even tell Sam why he hadn't asked him. Because Eliza had asked him not to. End of story.

Josiah thought about all the other men in town. There was young Zack, who helped Matthew in the saloon. He would undoubtedly be more reliable than Rawlins. Unfortunately, nobody respected the poor kid. And if no

6

one listened to him, then it wouldn't matter if he was responsible or not. What about that new fellow Clinton? What was his first name? When he was in town, he was always willing when Josiah asked him to help look for the cattle rustlers. Now that's a thought—Clinton.

Thinking about Clinton made Josiah think of the new Mills family who had just moved to town from the South. When he first saw their beautiful daughter, Mary Elizabeth, he thought he was in love. He snickered to himself. Yeah, love. The first time he talked to her, he knew she was not the one for him. Besides her beauty, she had a comely southern accent. Still, that wasn't enough for him.

Was anything enough for him? He wanted someone who had been around, maybe a little sophisticated, but also someone who could be happy in his little town. Was that too much to ask for? Did that woman even exist in this world? He hoped so.

Josiah exhaled in a huff and frowned. He was tired of being alone, that much was certain. Maybe more new families would move to Red Bluff. Word of his town and his lawmaking were getting around. A peaceful town with no gunfighters? Yeah, that's what everybody—except the gunfighters, maybe—was looking for. Maybe a bunch of women would come from outer space: all of them beautiful, sophisticated, and at home in his town— exactly what he was looking for—and he could have his pick! His laugh made the horse prick back his ears. Josiah stroked him on the neck. "It's okay, boy, I'm just amusing myself."

Outer space. Sometimes when he was in his bedroll at night, lying under the blanket of stars above him, he wondered if there was other life out there. How could there not be? So many stars, so many possibilities. It was arrogant to think we were the only intelligent life in this vast universe.

He wanted to hurry the horse toward home, but it had been a long trip. Ole Patches probably felt as tired as he was. And Bingo—he looked around for his dog—was tired as well. His tongue lolled out of his mouth. "You thirsty, Bingo?" Josiah motioned the horse to stop and swung off his back. He poured some water from the canteen into his hand and offered it to the dog. Bingo drank and then drank the second handful offered. Patches turned his head to look at the man and the dog. "Don't tell me you want to share my water, too, Patches! Aw, okay." He poured more water into his hand and offered it to the horse. When the horse refused, Josiah slurped it up himself. "Share and share alike."

Swinging back up into the saddle, he motioned the horse to continue. Less than a mile later, Josiah felt something strange with Patches' gait. He looked down at the horse's feet. "You limping, boy?" Josiah swung back off the saddle. He ran his hand down a front leg and picked up the horse's foot. "Dang! You lost a shoe!"

Shaking his head, he reached under his bedroll to get to the saddlebags. Retrieving a horseshoe, the small leather packet filled with horseshoe nails, and a small hammer, he bent over and set to work. Bingo, grateful for the rest and with his tongue still hanging from his mouth, relaxed in the shade. Patches, steady and docile as he was tough, stayed still until Josiah finished. Josiah straightened up and expelled a breath quickly. "Come on, now. Let's get back before the whole town is shot to hell." He replaced the packet and hammer and swung back onto the horse's back, urging the horse forward. If he had realized how prophetic his thoughts were, Josiah might have asked the horse to run home.

CHAPTER THREE

As THE MAN opened the heavy door to the stock truck, he looked up and saw the dark, heavy clouds approaching and the first snowflakes falling from the sky. He felt grateful the handful of cows he had were already safe inside the corral. Swinging the door open wide, he pulled the fence panels out of the truck and set them on the ground. Then he began putting them together in a circular fashion so the cows would load easier. He hooked up the last two panels to the ramp leading into the truck and then swung up easily onto his horse.

Opening the gate to the circular passageway, he rode the horse into the corral behind the cows. They mooed their discontent and milled around inside the small corral. Finally, he managed to guide one cow into the passageway, and the rest followed. When the heavy snow started to fall, all five cows were inside the truck. He quickly unsaddled his horse and put the saddle in the back. Then he unhooked all the panels and placed them inside, between the cows and where his horse would be. He led the horse inside and slipped off the bridle.

Back in the cab of the truck, he took off his snowy

jacket, lit a cigarette, and reached for his cell phone. The man chuckled to himself as he punched in the numbers. Five cows times five hundred dollars. Genuine grass fed beef! Twenty-five hundred dollars. Not bad for a day's work. And pure profit.

"Hey, Mac, I got 'em loaded. You ready for us?" After a pause, he continued. "Great, I'll see you soon." Another pause. "No, I don't have to go back tomorrow. Sheriff's outa town. Bye, now."

After starting the truck and letting it idle, he chuckled again before shifting it into gear. How lucky he was to have stumbled onto that cave!

CHAPTER FOUR

JENNA, MAGIC, AND Jet managed to get under the branches of a couple of trees that were close together. But the wind blew the snow so hard that it came at them sideways. Finally, Jenna motioned Magic forward to see if he could find a more sheltered spot. Then Jet started wiggling and wanting to get down. "Jet, what is it? That snow will freeze your little feet right off. And it's getting deep. Don't get lost."

With her nose to the ground, Jet walked several paces ahead. Jenna could barely see her. Then Jet barked. She disappeared for a minute, then came back and barked again. "Magic, I think Jet wants us to follow her. Let's go." Magic took a couple of tentative steps toward the dog. Jet barked again, and Jenna urged Magic forward. Less than five minutes later, they stood in front of what looked like a dark spot on a large rock. Jet disappeared inside it, then reappeared and barked again. "Keep going, Magic, maybe Jet discovered something here." Magic followed the dog inside what turned out to be a cave.

"Wow! No snow! You did it, Jet! Thank you! Now we

won't freeze to death." Jenna brushed the snow off herself. Taking off her hat, she shook it to get the snow off. Then she began brushing the snow off Magic. "We'll all be warmer now. Do you need help, Jet?" As if in answer, the dog shook herself free of snow. "Good girl!"

Time passed, and Jenna could still hear the wind whistling behind her at the mouth of the cave. Warmer now and bored, she thought maybe they could explore the cave and see what was there. Maybe she'd find some Indian ruins or rock art in here. She slid off Magic and walked slowly forward, in case there was a sudden drop-off. As she walked, she realized there was light up ahead. They walked toward it. The light came from a split in the rock above them, and snow filtered down. They backed up to keep out of the snow.

Jenna liked watching the snowfall, and it was peaceful in here. But soon she felt restless and wanted to explore what was on the other side of the snow. Enough light came from above that she could see the ground before her, so they kept up a good pace. Then she saw it. The opening. Smiling, she strode toward it, with Jet and Magic following. Strange, thought Jenna, it looks like sunshine. Maybe the snow stopped already. She turned around to see if snow still fell from the opening at the top of the cave, but the path had curved blocking the view. It was too far behind them anyway.

They walked out to the sunny sky. A few lazy clouds floated by, but not the kind that brings moisture. It must have stopped snowing—not unusual for a spring storm. The path did not look familiar. But after feeling trapped by the heavy snow, and then the close confines of the cave, Jenna was ready for a little exploring. She swung up on Magic's back and urged him forward on the trail.

Soon they reached a rutted dirt road that she didn't remember. Of course she had seen it before—her memory was just wacky from the fear of getting caught in the storm.

Turning right on the road, they continued until they came upon a wooden sign that said, Red Bluff, Colorado. Now, I know I haven't seen that sign before, thought Jenna. She ran her hand gently over the sign. It's hand-carved, I can still feel the marks. Weird, she thought, but urged the horse forward. It wasn't until a mile later that she realized there was no snow on the ground. Then she saw it!

Jenna grinned. She loved movie sets, and this one was excellent. It looked more authentic than any other she had seen. As she approached the town, she saw people in perfect period costumes going about their daily work. Whenever she had a chance, she always applied to be an extra anytime a movie was filmed in town. But she hadn't heard about this one.

With no one around to tell her not to, she slipped off Magic and draped his reins over the hitching post. "Jet, you stay here with Magic. Come on, get up." Jenna held out her hands, Jet jumped up, and Jenna boosted her onto the horse's back. Then, with a broad smile on her face, Jenna looked for a place to get some coffee. She still felt cold.

When she didn't find the catering truck that usually appeared at movie sets, she went to the next most logical place: the saloon. She walked through the swinging doors smiling and looked around in wonder at the authentic looking saloon. So absorbed in the realistic atmosphere of the place, she didn't notice all the looks people gave her. Making note of the piano, she thought that

14

Sarah would love this place.

She headed toward the counter. When she got there, she turned around and kept looking at the building, the people, and even the floor. They didn't spare a cent making this place look realistic. It looked real down to the smallest detail. And the people! The men. They were all hard-bodied, beautiful actors. The bartender was attractive, the twenty-something kid cleaning tables and serving drinks was attractive, all the men in the room were attractive, and the cowboy sitting at the bar a couple of seats down from her was gorgeous.

When she turned back toward the bartender to ask for a drink, the nearby cowboy spoke up. "Hey, woman who dresses like a man. I'll buy you a beer!"

Jenna looked down at her clothes. She wore jeans—not very period appropriate. "Oops, sorry, I left my dress at home. I can buy my own drink, thanks." Although no one said any different, she didn't know if she should be interacting with the actors. "I'll have a coffee," she said to the bartender, as she reached into her jeans for money. Pulling out a couple of dollars, she laid it on the counter.

"What are these?" said the bartender as he turned the money over in his hands. "I've never seen anything like these before."

The cowboy reached over and picked up a dollar. "Is this funny money, lady? You can get in trouble for that. Here, take your funny money back, and I'll buy you a coffee." He laid twenty-five cents on the counter, and the bartender gave him change. "I'm Eli. Nice to meet you."

"I'm Jenna," and she held out her hand.

Eli looked down, laughed, and then gave it a quick shake. "Funny clothes and funny acting, too. You're a strange one, Jane."

15

"No, not Jane. Jenna."

"Funny name, too. Here, sit beside me, Jenna."

She wrapped her hands around her hot coffee, inhaled the scent, and sighed. Looking at Eli, she said, "This feels so good, I feel like I just hit the lottery."

"Lottery? What lottery?" said Eli.

"Wow. You do stay in character, don't you?" Jenna looked around the room trying to find the camera. Before she could find it, someone rushing through the swinging doors interrupted her search.

"Eli," said a gruff voice. "It's time. Get your butt out here and face me like a man."

"Oh, leave off it, Will," said Eli. "I'm entertaining this pretty lady. I don't want to play your games." He turned back to Jenna.

"Nobody gets away with cheating me at cards," said Will.

"I beat you fair and square, Will. Leave me alone."

"I will leave you alone after we settle this." Will drew his gun from his holster, cocked it, and pointed it at Eli.

"Stop!" said the bartender, as he pulled a long barreled rifle from behind him and pointed it at the man with the gun. "Take this outside! I'll have no gunplay in here." And to a man leaning his head on a table, "Rawlins! Deputy Rawlins! Take care of this before it gets ugly." Then to the twenty-something kid, "Zack! Wake him up and get him on his feet."

Zack walked over and shook Rawlins. When he got no response, he pulled him up till he stood on his feet. But the man couldn't stand on his own. When Zack let him go, he slipped to the floor.

"Will, put the gun away, will you?" said Eli. "I'll come out and talk to you, and we can settle this like men. Put the gun away." To Jenna, he said, "I'll be back, ma'am. Wait for me."

Will put the gun into the holster and pushed through the swinging doors. Eli followed, shaking his head. Jenna took a sip of coffee, thinking this was part of the movie. When she noticed that everyone in the saloon followed the two men outside, she set down her coffee and went outside with them.

The two men stood thirty feet apart facing each other. Eli said, "Come on, Will, let's not do this."

Jenna, watching the scene with awe, clapped her hands! "Oh boy! A gunfight!"

"Pull your gun, Eli, or I'll shoot you where you stand."

Eli went for his gun, but wasn't quick enough for Will. A bullet went through his chest, and he fell to the ground. But he managed to lift his pistol up high enough to shoot at Will, hitting him in the arm.

Jenna jumped up and down. "Oh, that was so cool! That was so cool!" She ran to Eli and said, "That was great, Eli! Come back in now, and tell me where you learned to do that."

Puzzled and weak from loss of blood, Eli looked at her for a moment, and then his head fell back to the ground. Jenna put her hand under his head and tried to lift him up. Some blood got on her hand. "What the—?" said Jenna.

Suddenly, she stood up. "Oh no! It's real blood! It's real blood! What's going on here?" She began frantically wiping the blood on her jeans, trying to get it off her hands.

CHAPTER FIVE

CONTINUING DOWN THE trail, Josiah felt the horse's pace quicken. They must be getting closer to home. Patches was eager to get there, too. Shortly after that, Josiah saw the "Red Bluff" sign. Ah, finally, he thought.

Then Patches stumbled. "What's wrong, boy?" Josiah looked down and saw that one of Patches' other shoes was hanging on by a single nail. "Dang! So close to town. But I have to fix it." He swung off the saddle and retrieved the pouch of horseshoe nails from the saddlebags. "Luckily, you didn't lose this one, boy."

A couple of swift hammer strokes, and the shoe was back on securely. He swung back up on the horse, but didn't have to urge him forward. Patches wanted to get home as much as Josiah did. Several minutes later, Josiah heard the shots. When Patches felt his rider lean forward, he took off in a fast canter, with the dog following.

When Josiah arrived at the aftermath of the gunfight, swearing under his breath, what first drew his attention was the strange but beautiful woman, dressed in men's clothing, trying to pull up the man who was lying on the ground. New people in town, he thought. Then, when

18

the woman realized he was dead, she started sobbing and rubbing the blood off her hands. First things first, thought Josiah. He walked over to the woman and pulled her off the man. When she tried to wrap her arms around him, he pushed her away. "Not now, miss. Eliza!" he called to an older woman walking out of the Ralston General Store. "Eliza, come here!"

Eliza rushed over and threw her arms around the hysterical woman. She stroked her hair and tried to get her to calm down. Slowly, she moved them out of the street.

Josiah pushed with his boot at the man lying in the street to see if he would get a response. The man didn't move.

"He's cold as a wagon tire, Sheriff. I checked," someone said.

Then Josiah turned around to look at the other man who still stood with one hand on his pistol and the other hand holding a bleeding wound in his upper arm. "Get to the doctor, get it fixed, and get out of town. You're in the wrong place for these antics. You're not welcome here."

The man holstered his gun. And when someone directed him to the doctor's office, he walked away. Josiah looked over at Eliza and the strange woman. There had been a dog sitting atop a horse with no saddle, but now the dog was on the ground. The woman acted like she needed help getting on the horse. She stood there, grasping the mane with her head buried in the horse's neck.

"Zack, help her get up on that horse."

Although the young man walked over to help her, she shook her head and motioned him away from her. Then Josiah couldn't believe what he saw next. The horse knelt

19

down to allow the woman to climb on. When someone called him, Josiah lost track of her.

Walking back to the dead man, he said, "Yes, get him out of here. Take him up to the cemetery and get him buried.

"Where the hell is Rawlins? How did he let this get out of hand?"

Someone pointed toward the saloon. "I should have known," said Josiah. He walked toward the saloon and shoved the swinging doors open.

Rawlins was still lying on the floor where he had fallen. Josiah strode over and nudged him with his boot, none too gently.

"Whaaa? Whaaa?" said Rawlins.

"Get up, you no-account son of a something," said Josiah. "I asked you not to drink while I was away. Was that too much to ask, you worthless cuss?"

Rawlins struggled to a sitting position, leaned his head over, and vomited. "Sorry, Sheriff. What'd I miss?"

Josiah shook his head and pushed out of the saloon onto the street. He couldn't have this anymore. He just couldn't. Something had to be done, and he would do it right now. As he walked across the street toward the hotel, he mumbled to himself the whole way.

"Eliza? Eliza, I need to talk to you!" he said as he entered.

Eliza came out of the back room of the hotel. "Hallo, Josiah."

"Where's Samuel?"

"He's helping to bury that poor boy who was shot. I know what you want, Josiah, and the answer is still no."

Josiah pulled back his lips in a frown, shook his head slowly, and said, "Eliza. Listen to me. You know I won't go against your wishes, but I need Samuel right now. Look at what just happened. This would not have happened if Samuel had been my deputy. You know that."

"No, it wouldn't have happened, but maybe something worse would've happened. Maybe one of those hot heads would have shot Samuel. I'm sorry, Josiah, I can't take any more loss." Eliza put her head down, and tears started to flow. "No more loss. I can't survive it."

Josiah put his arms around the woman. "I'm sorry, Eliza, you're right. There is always risk there."

Eliza looked up. "Josiah, this is the first time you've had to leave town since you became sheriff. By the time you need to leave again, you'll have your new deputy. I'm sure of it." She patted his arm.

"If you say so, Eliza." He hugged her one more time and walked toward the door. Then he turned around. "Eliza, that woman you helped today. Did she say anything?"

"She said something funny. She said she thought it was a movie."

"What's a movie?" asked Josiah.

Eliza shrugged her shoulders. Josiah nodded his head and bounded out the door toward the doctor's office at the end of the street.

Josiah walked in, looked into the examining room, and saw the stranger sitting on the table with Doc bandaging his arm.

"How is he, Doc?"

"He'll be fine, good as new in no time. Just a flesh wound."

Josiah looked at the man on the table. "I wanted to make sure you understood me. I want you out of here immediately. When Doc finishes, you get on your horse and ride. Am I understood?"

The stranger didn't even look up. "Understood."

Josiah nodded his head once, turned, and walked out the door.

CHAPTER SIX

AFTER CLIMBING ONTO Magic's back, Jenna didn't have to ask him to take her home. He knew. She could always count on Ole Magic to do what she needed. Walking back through town was a blur, walking down the road was a blur, and walking through the cave was a blur. Jenna felt too traumatized to even wonder if walking back through the cave would take her back to her own time. The idea didn't even occur to her until she was back home again and in familiar surroundings. And next she knew Magic had stopped in the paddock by his stall. Jenna had sobbed all the way back.

Now, she slid off the horse. She led him back into his stall, made sure there was food in the automatic hay dispenser, and slipped the hackamore off his head. "I'm sorry, Magic, I can't take care of you right now. You have food, and you should be fine. I'll be out later. I have to go on in now and get myself out of these bloody clothes. I'm sorry."

Jenna struggled up the front stairs and into the house. As she hurried to the bathroom, she began tearing off her clothes. When she got there, naked, she turned on the shower full blast and stepped in. Her crying had still not stopped.

She didn't know how long she had been sitting on the floor of the shower when she heard Sarah's voice. The water had turned cold, and Jenna's tears had finally stopped. Sarah was her best friend, and had been walking into her house unannounced since she was sixteen, so it didn't surprise Jenna when she heard her.

"Jenna! What's going on? Where are you? What's this?" Sarah walked into the open bathroom holding a piece of Jenna's discarded clothing. She saw that Jenna sat inside the shower with the water pouring down. Jenna groaned.

Sarah slowly opened the shower door and saw Jenna on the floor with her arms wrapped around her knees. Feeling the cold water rushing out of the showerhead, she leaned over and turned it off.

"Jenna! Jenna, what's wrong?" She reached out to touch Jenna's arm. "Jenna! You're ice-cold! Let's get you out of there." Sarah grabbed a towel, helped Jenna stand up, and wrapped her in the towel. "Can you stand up okay?" When Jenna nodded, Sarah added, "I'm going to go turn on your electric blanket. Stand right here, I'll be right back!"

Jenna still stood in the same spot when Sarah returned. She helped her friend dry off and then helped her walk to the bedroom and get under the covers. "Here. Get under there. It should be a little warm now. Warmer than you, anyway. This isn't like you, Jenna. You're the rock. Will you tell me what happened?"

"First, would you mind giving Magic a quick rub down? I never miss doing that after a ride, but I couldn't today. Would you mind, Sarah?"

"Okay, you get warmed up, and I'll take care of Magic. This isn't like you, Jenna. You're the rock. Then you'll tell me what happened . . . right?"

Although the tears had stopped, Jenna's face was still streaked red from crying. Now the tears started anew. She nodded.

Fifteen minutes later, Jenna heard the front door open. And although she thought she had calmed herself down, before Sarah even got back into the room, Jenna started talking. "Oh, Sarah! It was terrible!"

"Wait, wait, wait," said Sarah. "What should I do with these?" She held up the clothes that she had picked up from the other room. Sarah was a neat freak.

"Oh, put them down! You'll get blood all over you! I'm just going to throw them away!" Sarah's clothes defined her. She wore better clothes than Jenna did, even when Jenna was practicing law. Sarah loved her clothes.

"Oh, these aren't my good clothes. Not to worry. Ew, that's blood? It'll wash. You don't have to throw them away."

"I never want to see that blood again! It was horrible, Sarah, horrible! It brought back all the old memories."

"I'm just going to rinse the blood out of these clothes now, and I'll be right back for the story."

"Sarah!" Sometimes Sarah's neatness got to Jenna. This was one of those times.

"Okay, okay, let me put them in the tub. I'll clean them out later." She disappeared into the bathroom and right back out again. "Now, a chair." She pulled a chair over to Jenna's bed and said, "Okay, I'm listening. Tell me everything."

Jenna started by describing the unexpected snowstorm, the cave, and seeing what she thought was a movie set.

"Oh! I love movie sets, too. What movie was it?" interrupted Sarah.

"No, Sarah, it wasn't a movie. Let me finish." Then Jenna described the saloon, the good looking cowboy, and the shootout. She ended the story when she left Magic in his stall.

"So the cave took you into the past?"

"Yes, exactly."

"How is that possible? Are you sure it was real?"

"The guy was definitely dead, Sarah. I'm sure."

"Wow, a time portal or something! That's cool."

"It wasn't very cool when that guy got shot right in front of me."

"Yeah, that would be a bummer," said Sarah. Then she brightened. "Did you say that the bar had a piano? And nobody was singing? Oh! Maybe I could get a singing job there!"

"I thought you loved your job, Sarah."

"What? Being a glorified secretary?"

"You're administrative assistant to the most senior partner in the law firm."

"Eh. Still a glorified secretary. Not exactly what I dreamed of when I was a girl. But being a singer *is* what I dreamed of! When can we go back?"

"I don't ever want to go back! It was horrible!"

"It was just horrible because that guy got shot. If no one gets shot, you'd go back, wouldn't you?" asked Sarah.

Jenna wanted to scream, "No!" as loud as she could. But, despite the man shot dead in front of her, she somehow knew that she would return. It was like she had to.

"I don't even know if the cave will work again. Maybe

it was just because of the snowstorm."

"Yes, but we can try! C'mon, Jenna, c'mon!"

"Okay, we'll go back," Jenna said quietly.

"What year do you think it was?"

"I have no idea. Old west. Shoot 'em up days."

"When can we go back? When?" shouted Sarah. "Tomorrow?"

"You have to work tomorrow."

"Oh, yeah. It's only Tuesday. I know. Who else can we invite?"

"Nobody," said Jenna quickly. "It should be a secret. I don't want it to get out."

"Oh come on, Jenna. Be a sport. How about your sister?"

Jenna thought for a moment. Her sister, Kat, would definitely enjoy the diversion. She and Kat had joined the Victorian Society together—a group of men and women who dress up in clothes from the 1800s.

"I'll call her," said Jenna.

"Oh, I'm so excited!" Sarah jumped up and clapped her hands. "I can't wait to go!"

CHAPTER SEVEN

AFTER TAKING CARE of his horse, Josiah was finally back in the sheriff's office. He walked around, checked the jail cells, opened the door to the room he slept in. Everything looked fine. At least Rawlins didn't mess the place up. Apparently he could do some things right.

Finally sitting in his own chair again, he leaned back and put his feet on the desk. It had been a long, tough day. He would just close his eyes for a minute.

Swirling images filled his dreams. The woman who wore pants was looking in his eyes and smiling. His arms were around her. That image blended with the next image of her sitting behind him riding the black horse bareback. They were flying over fences, and the horse was running faster, faster—

"Sheriff!"

Josiah woke with a start. "Oh, yeah, what, huh?" He blinked his eyes so he could focus on the man at the door. It was a rancher who had lost cattle before.

"Five more last night, Sheriff."

"Dang," said Josiah. "It has been awhile. And I thought maybe the rustler had moved on. I guess I know what I'll be doing tomorrow. I'll catch him eventually. Sorry that he's hit you twice now."

"I can't afford to lose many more cattle, Sheriff. None, really. This is going to hurt me."

"I'll do what I can and find him as soon as I can. You know what it's like. I can't make promises about this. I'm sorry."

Grumbling, the rancher walked out the door. Josiah yawned, and the images of the woman returned to his mind. *I've only seen her once, and I'm already dreaming about her? I need to get back to work!*

He closed the door of the office and walked back out into the street. Although he'd been gone less than two weeks, it felt like forever. This was home, and he missed it while he was away. Wanting to enfold himself into the town again, he decided to walk the streets.

As he walked past the school, he wondered about Annie the schoolmarm. Why wasn't he ever interested in her? Why, suddenly, was he so enamored of a strange woman wearing men's clothing? He didn't even know if she belonged to the man who got shot. *Think of something else, Josiah. Get your mind off her. You'll probably never see her again.* As he walked past the livery stable, he thought about what a pleasant little town Red Bluff was. It was his town. And he liked it here. He couldn't imagine ever leaving here.

Returning to the main street, he passed his office and found himself walking into the saloon. "Hallo, Matthew," he said to the bartender.

"If you're looking for Rawlins, he's not here," said Matthew.

"No, I was going to ask if you'd seen that Clinton feller around. More cattle are missing, and he's always

29

willing to help me look for them."

"He was here yesterday, spent the night at the hotel, but I haven't seen him today. Can I get you something, Sheriff?"

"No, thanks." Josiah turned to leave, then turned back. "You know that strange woman who wore pants? Did you see her earlier?"

"Yeah, she came in here for a coffee."

"Was she with the guy that got shot?"

"She had just met him. She tried to pay me with some weird looking paper money, so he bought her the coffee."

"Oh, okay, thanks." Josiah walked toward the door.

"You think she's involved in the cattle rustlin'?"

"No, I just—," he turned back to the bartender in time to see him grinning. Josiah shook his head and walked out the door.

CHAPTER EIGHT

IT SNOWED AGAIN all day Friday. Since she wasn't caught in it, Jenna thoroughly enjoyed the snow. It was a heavy, wet snow, and she had to slog through it on her way to the barn to feed the horses. But she was smiling.

After she had calmed down and after Sarah had left that night, Jenna lay in bed thinking of what she needed to do before they could return to the old Red Bluff. She *could* wear one of her Victorian Society dresses. But they were all spotless, and not what she wanted to wear on the back of a horse. So the following day, she had gone to the fabric store, bought some beautiful purple paisley denim, and a pattern for a long Victorian style dress.

Somewhere, she remembered, she had seen something about women in the "old days" wearing split skirts so they could ride horses. She couldn't find a pattern like that, but she knew adjusting wouldn't be difficult. Now, the dress was almost complete, and it was beautiful.

At seven o'clock, when Sarah was due to arrive, the front door bell rang. Jenna thought that was strange, because Sarah normally just knocked and walked in. Jenna opened the door. All she saw was a bunch of

31

clothes wrapped around two arms. Then she heard Sarah's voice.

"Help!"

Jenna grabbed some clothes from Sarah and asked, "Sarah, what *is* all this stuff?"

"I have to find the perfect dress for my job interview. Come out to the car with me, will ya, I have a few more loads."

"Sarah," Jenna said as they walked through the front door, "what job interview? What are you talking about? These are your Victorian clothes!"

"Jenna, I *really* want to sing at that saloon."

Shaking her head and smiling, Jenna said, "Oh, Sarah."

After both of them made two more trips out to the car, they finally had all the clothes inside. Jenna sat on a chair while Sarah straightened the mess up.

"I can't believe you have so many clothes! I have three Victorian outfits!"

"Well, if you want any of these, you can have them. As you can see, I have plenty!" When Sarah finished organizing, she walked to the kitchen to get a drink of water. On her way, she noticed Jenna's sewing machine out and the pretty purple dress draped over the back of the chair. "What's this? What are you doing?"

"Making a new dress for tomorrow. It's almost finished," said Jenna.

"Why do you need a new dress? Why not wear one of your Victorian Society dresses?"

"Those are my good clothes. This will be for my play clothes."

"They're all the same to me."

"With all this stuff, I can understand that. But don't

forget that you have to straddle a horse with the dress."

"Oh, that's right. Okay, let me go back through these and take out the ones that aren't full enough to go over my horse. That should make this a little easier."

"Why did you bring these over here?"

"So I can try them on—and you can help me decide which is the best wild west interview dress!"

"You're serious about this, aren't you, Sarah?"

Sarah turned around with a sober expression. "I've never been more serious, Jenna. I have always wanted to be a singer, and this is my chance."

"Okay, try something on, and let's decide."

After two hours of trying on dresses, they had three piles: definite no, maybe, and definite possibility. "Let's go back over the maybe's now. Do you need to rest first? I'm tired just watching you!"

"No," said Sarah. "I still have plenty of energy!"

An hour later, they ended up with ten in the possible pile. Sarah looked through them and took two of them out.

"You don't like those, after all?" asked Jenna.

"They're pretty, but not appropriate for a job interview—even if it is the 1800s."

Thirty minutes later, they had one picked out. The pink flowered dress was full enough so Sarah could get on and off her horse easily; it was pretty; and it was dressy enough for work, but not too dressy.

"Perfect!" said Sarah. "Now, what's next?"

"We need money," said Jenna. "They laughed when they saw my paper money. Where can we get some 1800s coins?"

"You're guessing on the 1800s, right?"

"Yes, but I feel sure that I'm close."

33

"I think there are a couple of coin dealers in town where we can buy some old coins. They're expensive, though," said Sarah.

"It won't take much. Eli gave the bartender a quarter for my coffee and got change. My guess is that ten dollars will go far."

"Oh! Where's Kat? I thought she was going to come with us."

"When I called her, she said she has to work tomorrow. She does want to go sometime, though."

"What time do you want to go?"

"It doesn't take long to get there, ironically," laughed Jenna. "I was thinking after lunch. I'm not sure if they have a restaurant or not."

"Okay, I'll go to the coin dealers in the morning and meet you back here at one."

CHAPTER NINE

AFTER MAKING THE final touches on her riding dress, Jenna prepared her lunch, leftover meat loaf and mashed potatoes. She stepped outside and nearly skipped all the way to the barn. Jenna didn't realize how excited she was about returning to the old west town.

Sarah had parked her car outside the barn. When Jenna walked in, she saw that Sarah already had her horse brushed and saddled.

"What!" Sarah, already dressed up, said. "You're not ready yet? I thought you'd be dressed, since Magic wasn't ready."

"Sarah, chill, we have plenty of time to get there. I'll brush and saddle Magic now, and then get dressed."

"No, I'm eager to get going. You put your dress on, and I'll take care of Magic. Which saddle do you want, your regular?"

"Yeah, the one with the scabbard attached."

"You're not taking your rifle, are you?" asked Sarah.

"Why not?"

"Someone might shoot you down! Don't forget where we're going! Or I should say, *when* we're going!"

"I'm sure I'll be fine, Sarah. Besides, I'm a fast shot!" joked Jenna. "I'll be right back."

Jenna put her dress on and slipped her cowboy boots back on. She was ready to head out the door when the phone rang.

"Hello."

"Jenna, I need to talk."

"Ryan, is this girlfriend troubles again?"

"Jenna, please. I need to talk about it."

"Ryan, I'm about to leave the house. Sarah is waiting for me in the barn. But I'll say this. If you'd choose women who had bigger brains and smaller breasts, you'd be a lot better off. Listen, I'll talk to you when I get home. Bye!"

Ryan was Jenna's younger brother. He had a bad habit of choosing the wrong women. Jenna could always see it coming, and she'd warn him. But he said he was ruled by his hormones, and then he'd move on ahead into yet another bad relationship. Many times she had told him that he was too old to let his hormones rule his head. Ryan was twenty-five years old—a few years younger than Jenna.

After the phone call, Jenna was back out to the barn in five minutes. "Let's go!"

"That was fast! I just finished saddling Magic. I'll get your hackamore."

Two more minutes, and they were out the back gate heading for a new adventure. They turned onto the main trail and kept going.

"Are we there yet?" asked Sarah.

"Sarah!"

Walking farther down the trail, Jenna noticed cow pies on the ground leading to another trail off to the right.

She was looking down the trail in that direction when Sarah spoke.

"Look, Jenna. Are any of your cattle missing? This is a strange place to see cow pies. There's no grazing here, is there?"

Jenna shook her head. "No, no grazing here. I was wondering about the cow pies myself."

"What's down that trail?"

"It leads to the street. There's an area where people can park their horse trailers, so they can get to the trail system. You know, not everyone is as lucky as I am to live right off the trail!"

"And as lucky as I am to have a friend who lives right off the trail!" said Sarah.

Several minutes more passed before anyone spoke. Then Jet barked. "Oh," said Jenna. "Jet just announced the turnoff. Let's go uphill for a while now.

"There's cow pies on this trail, too."

"Yeah, I saw that. Strange." After a few minutes going uphill, Jenna said, "Jet, don't let me miss the cave." Jet barked in response and ran ahead.

When Jet disappeared momentarily and then barked, Jenna turned Magic to follow the sound. Sarah trailed behind. A minute more, and the cave came into view.

"Is this it?" asked Sarah.

"Yup, let's go."

"It looks so ordinary. I thought it would be some super unusual place."

"Did you think it would have flashing lights and signs that said, 'Old West here!'?"

Sarah laughed and followed Jenna into the cave. They passed the light from above that Jenna remembered, only this time, no snow was falling. Another minute, and they were out the other side.

Sarah clapped her hands and spooked her horse. Sarah's horse was high-strung, just like Sarah, thought Jenna.

Not even noticing her horse's behavior, Sarah said, "I'm so excited! I'm so excited! Oh, look, more cow pies."

"Well, we're in the old west now, there's no telling where they graze cattle here."

They turned onto the main road. Silence followed as they both looked around in wonder. It would take a long time before Jenna took this old west town for granted. What? That made it sound like she would return. Wasn't this trip just to show Sarah? Or was it?

The sign made Sarah clap her hands again which made her horse shy to the side again. "You didn't tell me it was a hand carved sign that said, 'Red Bluff,' did you?"

"I thought I did, but maybe I forgot. The town's just up ahead."

When the town came into view, Sarah shook her head and said, "I can see why you thought it was a movie set. It looks fantastic! Just out of an old western. Where's the saloon?"

They dismounted from their horses in front of Ralston General Store. That left plenty of room between them and the other horses tied in front of the saloon. Sarah's horse wasn't as docile as Magic, so she removed his bridle and put on the halter and lead rope that she had brought. She attached the rope to the hitching post. Jenna took a blanket from her saddlebags and put it on top of her saddle. Then she asked Jet to jump up. She didn't want Jet's sharp claws putting holes in her good saddle.

"Let's check out the general store," suggested Jenna as she walked toward the door.

Sarah grabbed her arm and gently pulled her toward the middle of town. "Oh, no, you don't. We're going directly to the saloon! You can look at the store later. Where's the saloon? Oh I see it! I see it! Let's go!"

Sarah quickened her pace, and Jenna tried to keep up. When they arrived at the saloon, Sarah gave an exaggerated push to get the swinging doors open. "This is so cool."

"I don't think they use the word 'cool' in the old west. Shhhh."

Sarah looked around the room, saw the piano, and gasped. Then she walked directly to the bar. Jenna looked quickly around and saw someone who looked vaguely familiar at the end of the bar. He was handsome, with blue eyes and dark hair. While she walked up to the bar to sit beside Sarah, she saw the bartender look at the familiar man and motion in her direction.

The bartender approached Sarah and said, "What can I get for you two beautiful ladies?"

"Hey, handsome," said Sarah.

"Easy," said Jenna under her breath. "Keep talking like that, and they'll think you're a painted lady, or whatever they call those women."

That didn't daunt Sarah. "Barkeep? Is that what you're called here?" Sarah asked.

"Some call me Barkeep, others call me Matthew. And you are?"

"My name is Sarah!"

"Sarah, pleased to meet you." Matthew leaned over and kissed Sarah's hand.

"Oh, I love this place already!"

"What can I get for you two pretty ladies?""

"Do you have sarsaparilla?" asked Sarah.

Matthew turned back to the counter behind the bar. "One sarsaparilla coming up!"

"Make that two!" said Jenna. "How did you know—" She didn't get to finish her question because the familiar man stepped up to the seat next to hers.

"How are you, ma'am? Are you all right? You were right upset last time I saw you," said Josiah.

Oh, thought Jenna. He was the man who pulled her off Eli. Who was he? "Yes, I'm fine now. It was just a—a shock to find that man dead." Jenna kneeled down to pet the dog at his heels.

"That's Bingo. Just so you know, ma'am, that kind of thing normally doesn't happen in my town, but I was gone for a couple of weeks."

Jenna straightened up to face him. "Your town?"

"Oh, beg your pardon, ma'am. My name is Josiah Stone. I'm the sheriff." He pointed to his badge.

Jenna put out her hand to shake his and then immediately drew it back. "Oh! I didn't see your badge. My name is Jenna Leyton."

"Nice to meet you, Miss Jenna Leyton," nodding his head. "Unless it's Mrs. Leyton?"

"No, no, just me. I'm not married," said Jenna. "And this is my friend, Sarah James."

"Hallo, Miss James. My pleasure." He nodded his head and tipped his hat."

"Nice to meet you, Sheriff."

Turning back to Jenna, the sheriff said, "Are you new in town, Miss Jenna Leyton?"

Jenna quickly glanced over at Sarah and gently shrugged her shoulders. "Um, well, not exactly new, but yes, kind of new."

The sheriff smiled. "That's clear as mud! Well, I'll leave you two ladies alone now," he said and walked back to the end of the bar. When he got there, he turned back to look at Jenna.

"He's handsome," whispered Sarah. "And he's still looking right at you."

Jenna turned toward the end of the bar and smiled at the sheriff. "So is the bartender, Sarah." She had noticed that Sarah had not taken her eyes off the bartender since they arrived. Maybe she should give Sarah time to make her plea for a job. She took one more sip of her delicious sarsaparilla and walked over to where the sheriff was sitting.

"Sheriff, who was that woman who helped me that day? I'd like to thank her."

"Miss Jenna Leyton, you can call me Josiah."

"Thank you, Josiah, and you can call me Jenna."

"Well, Jenna, that was Eliza. She and her husband, Samuel, run the hotel across the street." When Jenna turned around to look out the window and looked confused, Josiah added, "Here, I can show you." He took her arm and led her out the door and into the street.

Jenna liked the feel of his hand on her arm. It was firm but tender. When he took it away as they crossed the street, she immediately felt a small loss.

"Eliza said that you thought the shooting was a movie. What's a movie?"

"Oh," said Jenna, trying to figure out how to explain that. "It's, ah, it's, I don't know how to explain it. But, anyway, I was wrong." She smiled up at him and hoped that would be the end of it.

Neither Jenna nor Josiah noticed the curtain move as

they approached the hotel. "Well, this is it. You can find your way from here," said Josiah, as he pointed at the hotel door.

"Thanks, Sheriff. Oops, I mean, Josiah." She walked the rest of the way across the street and put her hand on the doorknob. As she opened it, she turned to see that Josiah still stood in the street watching her. She smiled at him and walked into the hotel.

CHAPTER TEN

SHERIFF JOSIAH STONE stood in the middle of the street watching Jenna walk into the hotel and trying to catch his breath. When he had put his hand on her arm to lead her out of the saloon, he hadn't wanted to remove it. Then he thought it might be making her uncomfortable, so he had forced it down to his side.

What was happening to him? Big brave Sheriff Josiah Stone. That's how people referred to him. He didn't feel brave right now. He felt like an adolescent with his first crush. But his first crush didn't feel like this. Nothing had ever felt like this. And he didn't even know her! What was going on?

He took a deep breath and returned to the saloon. Sitting at the end of the bar again, he ordered a beer, thinking that talking to Matthew would distract him from these unfamiliar feelings. But Matthew was deep in conversation with Jenna's friend, Sarah.

Josiah took the beer and sat at a table away from the bar. Why was he feeling this way? Who was this Jenna Leyton anyway? She couldn't even answer simple questions, like what a movie was and if she was new to town.

Where was she from anyway? And why oh why did she have such a hold on him after just meeting her? It wasn't just her beauty, although her dark hair and emerald green eyes were attractive. He finished the beer and decided to walk around town. That usually settled him down after a bad conflict with Rawlins. Maybe it would work with this, too.

Stepping out of the bar, he immediately looked around. Where was her horse? Oh, there it was, saddled this time, and in front of the store. There was a rifle on the saddle! What in the world was a woman doing with a rifle?

That woman was a mystery! From wearing men's clothes the first time he saw her, to not giving him straight answers, to a rifle on her saddle—a total mystery. Was he attracted to her because she was a mystery? No, he thought. He was attracted to her *despite* her being a mystery.

Glancing at the hotel, he couldn't see through the windows and didn't know what was going on in there. Why did she want to see Eliza? Questions and more questions. And no answers. And still the feeling persisted. Walk, Josiah, walk. That will get your mind off her.

But it didn't. He glanced across the street at the school. Sometimes, he liked to stand at the back of the classroom and watch Annie and the children. He liked kids. But it was Saturday and no school. Why didn't he like Annie? She was attractive and smart. But she didn't appeal to him. Nobody appealed to him like Jenna.

This was crazy! She might leave today, and he'd never see her again. Then what would do with these feelings? What would he do with them anyway, if she didn't feel the same? Crazy thoughts! What was he thinking? Meet a woman once, get down on one knee, and declare his undying love for her? He didn't think so!

Walking around the corner, he opened the door to Doc's office, thinking he could talk to him for a while. But Doc had somebody in there with him talking about a sore throat. He didn't need that. He already had a sore head from thinking about this woman.

Continuing around the block, he eventually came full circle and ended up in front of the store. The black horse was there, this time with a saddle, standing next to a bay. Josiah stepped up to the black horse and held out his hand. The horse nickered, and the dog, sitting on a blanket on the saddle, wagged his tail. Both of them friendly, that's good. He rubbed the horse's neck and then stepped over and petted the dog. "So what do you think? Do I have a chance with your owner?"

Stepping back onto the wooden sidewalk, Bingo looked up at him. "Don't worry, boy. You're my dog. You'll always be my dog! But wouldn't you like to have a friend?" Josiah looked at the dog sitting on the blanket on top of the horse's back.

He took a deep, refreshing breath, tried to push thoughts of the woman from his mind, and walked through the door into his office.

CHAPTER ELEVEN

Eliza stood at the front desk speaking to someone. Jenna didn't want to disturb her, so she turned away and looked around the hotel. The floors were hardwood, but mostly covered with rugs. To her left, the front desk was against the middle of the wall. A door was at the end closest to the front, and a staircase began at the far side of the front desk. Up the staircase, the second floor had a balcony that surrounded three sides. To her right was an open door. She walked over to it and peered in. It was the restaurant.

When someone touched her on the shoulder, she turned around. It was Eliza, an older woman, pretty, with gray streaks in her hair.

"Are you all right, child? Last time I saw you, you were in a bad way."

"I'm fine now, Eliza. Thank you so much. I needed a shoulder to cry on, and you were right there. Thank you."

"Oh, no need to thank me, dear, that's just what I do. But you have me at a disadvantage. You know my name, and I don't know yours."

"I'm sorry. My name is Jenna Leyton." Jenna refrained from extending her hand this time.

"Eliza McKenna. Pleased to meet you." The woman turned around and walked toward the door by the front desk. "Come on, Jenna, dear, let's sit a spell."

"No need for that, Eliza, I came over to thank you for helping me."

"Oh, need smeed, child, come sit with me. It's not often that I have someone new and interesting to talk to."

Jenna followed her through the door. Inside was a sitting room with an eating area to the side. She could see through the door to another room that looked like a kitchen.

"That's not the kitchen for the restaurant, is it?" asked Jenna and was immediately sorry that she had asked. Back in these old days, they might not have thought to put the kitchen close to where they were serving.

"Oh, no, the restaurant kitchen is on the other side of the building. Much bigger. This one is all mine, where I cook for the family. My mother insisted on it after another fire burned this place down for the second time."

"The hotel burned down twice?" Jenna asked.

"Not just the hotel. The whole town. Twice. Did you notice how there are a few feet between buildings? They decided to do that after the second fire. And after two murderers escaped, hundreds of dollars burned up, and all the mail was destroyed during the second fire, they built the jail, the bank, and the post office out of bricks. And then my mother insisted the builders use brick for our hotel, too."

Suppressing the urge to say "wow" thinking that "wow" wasn't used in the nineteenth century, Jenna said,

47

"That's interesting."

Eliza sniffed the air. "Sometimes I can still smell the smoke. Can you smell it?"

Jenna sniffed the air. She glanced at Eliza, then quickly looked away. "No, Eliza. I don't mean to sound rude, but it's your imagination."

"Jenna, dear, your eyes just got a faraway look in them. Would I be wrong in guessing that you're speaking from personal experience?"

"Sometimes when I'm in my new barn, I can smell the burning." Jenna hesitated. "It was all cleaned up really well, and no one can smell it but me." Jenna blinked away the tears and looked at Eliza. "Yes, very personal."

Eliza, seeing the emotion in the woman's eyes, patted her hand. "Do you want to talk about it, dear?"

"No. Yes, I do." As soon as she said yes, the tears began to flow. She didn't stop them this time. "No one knows exactly what happened, but the best guess is that my parents' barn started burning. My parents raised show horses. They ran out to the barn to save the horses from the flames, but it was too late. They only managed to get two horses out—my horses—and when they went back in to get the other horses, the roof of the barn fell in on them. My parents and the rest of the horses all perished."

Eliza patted Jenna's hand but didn't say a word. She just waited while Jenna caught her breath.

"I feel so guilty that they died saving my horses. So guilty." Jenna slowly shook her head.

"Jenna, they went back in to save their horses. It would have happened anyway."

"But maybe if they had saved theirs first, they wouldn't have had to go back in."

48

"Jenna, it's what parents do. They do it for their children." This time Eliza got a faraway look in her eyes. "Parents would do anything to save their children from heartbreak, anything. And it sounds like your parents loved their horses—they would have gone back in to save them, regardless, don't you think?"

"Yes, I think you're right. Those horses meant everything to them." She wiped away her tears and looked at Eliza.

The older woman stood up and said, "Here, let me get you a handkerchief."

"No, it's okay, Eliza. I'm all right now." Jenna wiped away more tears and smiled at Eliza. "This is the first time I've told anyone how guilty I feel. Thank you for listening."

"No need to thank me, Jenna. I told you, anytime you need a shoulder to cry on, come to me!"

Jenna reached over and squeezed the woman's hand. "Thank you." She stood up. "I should be getting back now. My friend will wonder where I ran off to."

Eliza stood up and glanced out the sitting room window to the building across the street. As Jenna walked toward the door, she followed. Jenna stopped at the window and looked out expectantly.

Eliza noted that and said, "Jenna, dear, I've enjoyed our talk so much. Why don't you come to supper next Friday? I'd love to have my husband, Samuel, meet you."

Jenna turned around to face Eliza. "Eliza, I'd love to." She put her hand on the doorknob, then turned back to Eliza. "Oh, I don't think I can. I don't want to ride all the way home in the dark."

"Nothing you have to worry about, my dear. You will stay here."

49

"Oh, I couldn't possibly intrude—"

"Dear, this is a hotel. You are welcome to stay here."

Jenna smiled. But, after thinking a second, looked concerned.

"What is it, dear? Tell me."

"Oh, my dog. I never go anywhere without her."

"We're dog people, Jenna. Look." Eliza pointed to the wall across from the front door. There lay a tired old cocker spaniel-looking dog, his ears floppy, and his muzzle grizzled with gray. "Your dog is welcome here."

Jenna, overwhelmed with the woman's hospitality, hugged her. "Thank you, Eliza. And thank you for listening to my story."

"It's what I do, Jenna. It's what I do."

Jenna opened the door, but turned when Eliza spoke again.

"Jenna? I'll invite Josiah, too . . . "

Jenna smiled at the older woman and walked out into the street.

CHAPTER TWELVE

ONCE IN HIS office, Josiah didn't know what to do with himself. He went over the papers on his desk, but mostly just moved them from one side to the other. Then he dragged out the file of wanted posters. Looking at each picture trying to memorize it didn't work. All he saw in the faces was her face. Her face on a wanted poster. Yes, he wanted her. He didn't even know her, and he wanted her.

Josiah tried to focus on the pictures again and decided to check the front window to see if she had left the hotel yet. Then he sat back down to look at the posters again. A thought occurred to him, and he picked up the posters. He could look through them just as easily standing at the window, and then he would see when she left the hotel.

The posters weren't blurring into her face anymore, but he couldn't concentrate on them at all. Where was she? All she wanted to do was thank Eliza. What's taking her so long in there? No sign of her out the window.

Disgusted with himself, he put the posters back on his desk. Any of those "bad guys" could walk down the street and say hallo to him, and he wouldn't recognize them. The image of her filled his mind. Jenna. The name suited her. Enigmatic and different.

Maybe he'd go back to the saloon. Since her friend was there, she had to return. He could wait for her there. Wait and do what?

Brave Sheriff Josiah Stone felt like a schoolboy. He had had women before. And he had even fancied a girl or two, but in all his years he had never felt *this* before. He couldn't think! And again he had to tell himself that it was possible that she would leave today, and he'd never see her again.

Movement down the street caught his eye. The hotel door swung open, and Jenna emerged. Josiah nearly fell over himself getting out the door. Swiftly, he walked down the street and met her in front of the saloon.

Trying to be nonchalant, he said, "Oh, hi. How did your thank-you go?"

"Very well. Eliza is a wonderful person."

"That was a very long thank-you!"

"Oh, well. We bonded."

"Bonded? What's bonded?" The woman was a mystery he thought.

"Oops. Sorry. Um, we got along really well and had some things in common."

Josiah turned toward the saloon doors. "Shall we go in?"

"Sure." Jenna smiled up at him, and he almost fell down.

They walked in through the swinging doors to the sound of Jenna's friend, Sarah, playing the piano and singing "Oh Susanna." She had a good voice. Josiah pointed to a table where they could watch Sarah, and then he held the chair for Jenna.

When Sarah finished "Oh Susanna," Josiah said, "Your friend has a good voice."

"She does. This is her job interview, I suppose."

"Job interview?"

"Oops, sorry, I mean—"

"I know what a job interview is, Jenna. I don't know what you mean by it."

Jenna breathed easier. "Oh, good. I didn't know how I was going to explain that one. Sarah wants to sing in this bar. She thought maybe the bartender—what's his name? Michael?—would hire her."

"Matthew. Matthew Pelletier. I'm sorry for your friend, but I don't think Matthew has the money to pay someone to sing. That's why the last person left."

"I'm sorry to hear that. It will disappoint Sarah. She's always wanted to be a singer, and she thought this would be her chance."

Josiah shrugged his shoulders and tried to be sympathetic, but he didn't say anything because Sarah had started singing again. It was a pretty song, but he didn't recognize it. Something about living on the range.

He looked at Jenna, and she was smiling. And he noticed that she was mouthing the words as Sarah sang. Maybe it was popular where they came from, wherever that was. Josiah was about to bring up the subject again, when Sarah stopped singing, strolled over to their table, and sat down.

"That felt great! I love singing!"

"You're a great singer, Sarah," said Josiah. He noticed that Jenna didn't say anything to her friend, just looked at her with a sad face. She felt bad for her friend. Josiah liked that; he liked a woman who was compassionate. In fact, he liked everything about her.

"Well, Jenna, are you ready to go back? I'm tired."

"Sure, let's go." Jenna stood up.

"I'll be right back," said Sarah. "I want one more sarsaparilla. They are great! Do you think they have plastic to-go cups?"

Josiah didn't know what Sarah meant, but he noticed that Jenna gave her a dirty look. He didn't want her to get away. Not yet. Not till he found out more about her.

"So, Jenna, will you be coming back to town any time soon?"

She grinned broadly, and her eyes sparkled. "Yes, next Friday. Eliza asked me to supper."

Josiah smiled in return. "Well, I guess you two did do the bonding then!" In his mind he was already trying to figure out how to wrangle an invitation from Eliza. It shouldn't be difficult. Eliza and Samuel were like parents to him. He'd just tell her how he felt about Jenna. No! He couldn't do that, not when he didn't even understand it himself.

"Josiah?" Jenna said when she saw the distant look in his eye. "Where'd you go?"

"Oh, sorry, Jenna. Well, maybe we'll run into each other again. Good day!" He tipped his hat to her and pushed open the saloon doors.

Josiah dashed across the street trying not to run. Grabbing the door handle of the hotel, he burst inside and immediately started calling to Eliza without noticing if she was busy or not.

"Eliza! Eliza!"

"Josiah! No need to crash in here like a cowboy fresh off the range! Now, what is it, lad?"

"Eliza, could I possibly, I mean would you mind if I

came to supper with you next Friday night?"

"Well, Josiah, I just don't know. Samuel and I are having company that night."

"Yes, I know, and I thought, maybe——"

She chuckled and interrupted him. "Oh, stop your groveling, Josiah. I had always intended to invite you. Josiah Stone, I do believe you're smitten!"

Josiah's eyes sparkled. He grabbed Eliza and picked her up in a big hug. "Thank you, Eliza!" And he turned to walk out the door.

"Josiah!"

Josiah turned back. "Yes, Eliza?"

"You come crashing in here like a cowboy and leave the same way without saying good-bye!"

"Oh no!" exclaimed Josiah.

"What now?"

"I didn't say good-bye to Jenna!"

"Well, hurry and you can still catch her."

"Good-bye, Eliza, and thank you!" said Josiah, as he raced out the door. He saw Jenna and Sarah at the edge of town, so he ran down toward the end of the street. When he thought he might be close enough, he called out, "Good-bye, Jenna!"

When she turned around to wave, he returned the wave and then added, "See you on Friday!" He stepped into his office with a wide, beaming smile. She was coming back! And he was going to have supper with her! Well, with Eliza and Samuel and her, but still—she was coming back. He'd see her again! He leaned back in his chair and kept smiling.

CHAPTER THIRTEEN

As Jenna and Sarah approached the edge of town, she heard Josiah. She turned around and saw him waving. He shouted, "Good-bye" and "See you Friday!" So there was no reason to wonder why he left so abruptly a few minutes before. She did think it was strange when she saw him rush across the street to the hotel after she told him Eliza had invited her to dinner.

Sarah interrupted her thoughts. "Who was that?"

"Josiah."

"Who? Oh, the handsome sheriff. He likes you."

"He's handsome and nice," said Jenna.

"Handsome and nice? You haven't said that about anyone since you broke up with Daniel. You like him!"

"Well, he is handsome and nice."

"And one hundred or more years in the past! Jenna, get real! If you're ready for a new man, find one in your own time."

Jenna looked at her disapprovingly. "Sarah, if you want a real singing job, find one in your own time."

"Oh. Point taken. He is handsome."

"So is Matthew, the bartender! How was it talking to

him? I'm sorry you didn't get the job."

"What makes you think I didn't get it?"

"Josiah told me that Matthew doesn't have the money to pay an entertainer. That's why the last singer left."

"Well, that much is true. But I asked if I could work for tips, and he said yes! So, it's a go! I start Friday night. I'm spending the night at the hotel across the street, and then I'll sing Saturday night, too. I'm jazzed about this! It's what I've always wanted!"

"Good for you, Sarah. I'm glad it's working out. I'll see you at the hotel Friday night!"

"What do you mean?"

"Eliza—remember I told you about that woman who hugged me after the shooting—I went to thank her, and she invited me to supper next Friday night!"

"Cool! We can stay in the same room! It will be fun! Oh! Unless you want to stay with the handsome sheriff."

"It's a little early for that, Sarah. Here's the turnoff. Follow Jet."

Jet led them back into the cave. Halfway through it, Sarah said, "Hey, look at that. A fence panel." She pointed to the side of the cave in a darkened area.

"I see it. That is curious. The cow pies and now the fence panel. Strange. Maybe I'll mention it to Josiah."

"Yeah, right, and tell him how you're from a hundred years in the future. Hey, did you find out what year it was?"

"No, and I guess you didn't either."

"No, I didn't. I was too involved in singing."

"Oh, by the way, Josiah wasn't familiar with 'Home on the Range.' I could tell the way he looked when you sang it."

"I was having a hard time coming up with songs that I

thought were fitting. I'll have to look some up on the internet. But it will make it more difficult that I don't know the year yet."

"Well, look up 'Home on the Range,' and it's before that. That should help a little!"

Sarah nodded her head, and they rode in silence for several minutes. Then Sarah said, "You really like that sheriff?"

"I think I do, yeah."

"I'm happy for you, Jenna. I hope it works out."

"You weren't interested in Matthew at all? He kissed your hand! He seemed interested."

"Oh, you know, I have too much going on in my own life to think about a man right now."

"Sarah."

"Yes?"

"I know about Marcus." Marcus was Sarah's boss. Jenna had long known that Sarah was in love with him. Although Sarah had tried to hide it, it was too obvious to miss.

Sarah turned quickly to face Jenna. "How long have you known?"

"I've known since you started working for him."

Sarah shook her head and wiped a tear out of her eye. "I can't help it, Jenna. He is so smart and so handsome. I just love him."

"He's so married, Sarah, and he's not the type to screw around. Daniel and I used to socialize with them. They're happily married. You can see it in their eyes when they're together."

"I didn't want to screw around—I hoped that he would fall in love with me and leave her. Silly, huh."

"Who knows the way of the human heart? You need

to try to let him go and find someone real to fall for."

Sarah laughed. "You mean like someone who lived a hundred years ago!"

Jenna smiled, and they rode on. In a few more minutes, they were back to her ranch, putting the saddles away and brushing down the horses.

CHAPTER FOURTEEN

THE FOLLOWING DAY, five ranchers exploded into Josiah's office like dynamite and went off right in front of him. With all of them shouting at once, it was difficult to decipher what they were even talking about. But he recognized them. They were the ones hardest hit by the cattle rustler. The rustler had been operating for a few months, taking four, five, or six cows at a time, once every week or two. And Josiah didn't have a single clue about who it was or where he was taking the cattle. Now the ranchers were furious, and he couldn't blame them.

Josiah held up his arms. "Okay, stop!" When they kept shouting, he yelled, "Quiet!" Then he shouted louder and louder to try to get their attention. He was tempted to take out his gun and shoot into the ceiling, but it had taken months to fix the hole the last sheriff made up there. "QUIET!"

Still mumbling and grumbling, they quieted down. "Okay, gentlemen. I understand your concerns, and I understand that you can't take more of these losses. But there aren't any clues! What do you expect me to do?" When they all started talking again at once, Josiah held up his arms and said, "One at a time, please!"

After five more minutes and a few more requests of "one at a time," he finally understood. They wanted him to come to each of their ranches and reinvestigate to see if he—or they—had missed anything that might help him catch the rustler. That sounded reasonable, and Josiah agreed. Since the ranchers were in various directions and distances from town, starting tomorrow he would ride out to each ranch and look for anything that he had missed before.

The ranchers left, still angry, but more calmed down. And Josiah had miles of riding to do in the next few days. He only hoped all the riding and revisiting where the cows were stolen from would net him a solution to the rustling. Right now, it was like the cows were just disappearing. And what would happen if he couldn't find anything—couldn't find the guy responsible for the rustling? Would the ranchers run him out of town? Probably not, but he hoped he would find something so he didn't have to find out.

And one rancher, the one closest to town, had a wife who did sewing on the side. He could talk to her and see if he could get a new shirt in time for Friday's dinner. That would work out great if he could arrange it.

There was another reason he wanted to go to the ranch south of town first. He wanted to see if he could figure out where Jenna came from.

Next morning after first light, Josiah headed out. In his saddlebags was some food that Eliza had prepared for him. It would be a long, tedious day. Josiah knew that some ranchers back east had begun fencing in their cattle with various means, but it hadn't caught on here. So what he was looking at in the next few days was riding acres and acres of open range, and looking where the ranchers *suspected* the cows had disappeared. And where the loss really occurred could be acres away from where they thought. So Josiah didn't expect any huge revelations this week, although he did hope for one.

On the way to the first ranch, Josiah noticed what looked like a deer trail veering off to the left. A deer trail with big deer and some horse manure to boot. He turned Patches onto the trail. A few minutes later the trail ended at what looked like a cave. Did his beautiful Jenna live in a cave? That made him laugh.

"Jenna? Jenna, you in there?" No answer. He returned to the main trail.

At the first ranch, he was successful in that the rancher's wife agreed to make him the shirt by Friday. But after riding out to where the rancher suspected the loss took place, and then going back and forth over most of his property, Josiah found nothing.

The second, third, and fourth day, he covered miles of territory with no results at all. Thursday evening, he lay in bed thinking about his week and thinking about seeing Jenna the following day. Although he was too tired to feel excited, he went to sleep with a smile on his face at the prospect of seeing her again.

Friday morning, he got up extra early and was on the road before first light. Patches and Bingo didn't understand, but they didn't say anything. The ranch was bigger than he had expected, but luckily he didn't have to ride the whole property. He found something! It was Bingo who brought it to his attention. The dog sniffed at something in the dirt, and Josiah dismounted to see what it was. Josiah picked up the object and knew it meant something. He just didn't know what.

CHAPTER FIFTEEN

JENNA SLEPT WELL that night and dreamed of horses, cowboys, and kind motherly figures. She knew the fabric store and coin store were closed Sunday, but there was something else she wanted to do, anyway.

After breakfast, she was about to go out to the barn to get Magic, when the phone rang. It was her brother, Ryan.

"Do you have a few minutes to talk, Jenna?"

"I'm about to go riding, you wanna go?"

"No, I've got plans today. Can we just talk for a few?"

"Sure, Ryan. What's up? What did Trinity do now?"

"Tiffany. You won't believe this one, Jenna. I asked her if she would consider quitting her job and helping me in the store. You know what she said?"

Jenna rolled her eyes and wished that Ryan were in the same room so he could see them roll. His stories about women were all the same. Either the woman took advantage of him in a bad way, or the woman said or did something too stupid to believe. So she knew where this was going.

"What did she say, Ryan?"

"She said she couldn't work for me because she had her career to think about!"

"She's a clerk in a department store!"

"I know!"

"So, Ryan, when are you going to get rid of this one?"

"Not today. We're driving up to the mountains for dinner."

"Someplace expensive, I'll bet.

"Well, yeah. Someplace she found on the internet that she wanted to try."

Exasperated, Jenna said, "Ryan, why don't you—"

Then she decided that it wasn't worth the effort. He wouldn't listen anyway. "Ryan, you want to go riding sometime? I've got something really cool to show you."

"Yeah, sometime. Listen, Jenna, I have to run now. Good talking to you. Bye."

"Bye, Ryan." Jenna smiled and shook her head. There was no getting through to that guy. He had to learn his lessons by himself.

What was she doing before that frustrating phone call? Oh, yeah. Her investigation. She walked to the barn to brush Magic. When she finished, she slipped on his hackamore and led him out of the barn. In one fluid motion, she swung up on his back and guided him to the back gate.

Once they were on the main trail, she began looking for the cutoff, because she wasn't sure where it met the main trail. She turned onto it and discovered plenty of cow pies. They reached the end less than ten minutes later. While Jet sniffed the ground, Jenna and Magic walked around close to the parking area.

Jenna found what she was looking for. It looked as if someone had set up some fence panels by the parking area. Inside a roughly circular area, were piles of cow pies. Putting it all together—the cow pies *and* the fence panel in the cave, and now this—but why?

Satisfied with her investigation, although not with the reasoning behind it, she asked Magic to take her home. Back in the barn, she gave him a quick brush down and returned to the house.

Jenna spent the rest of the afternoon on her computer searching for old west fashions and random facts about the old west. She turned in early and fell right to sleep.

Next morning, after feeding the horses, Jenna drove into town. First stop was the fabric store to buy a new pattern and more fabric. She had decided that since she was spending the night, she could make a dress that wasn't a riding dress. Then pack the new dress, and wear the riding dress she already had for the ride there and the way back. She found some beautiful multi-shaded green material and bought the pattern she had found on the internet the day before.

Then she drove to the thrift store. She didn't know what she could pack her overnight gear in. A backpack came to mind, but she didn't think they had those back in the "old days." So she checked the thrift store shelves for something more suitable. After a few minutes of searching, she found two: a smaller one for her and a bigger one for Sarah. Knowing Sarah, she'd bring a ton of stuff.

Her last stop before going home was the coin store. Jenna wasn't sure which store Sarah had gone to, so she stopped at the one on the way home. The gold coins were outrageously expensive. But with the prices in the old west, she thought she could make do with some silver dollars, half dollars, and quarters. She bought two hundred dollars worth that were mostly half dollars and quarters. Most silver dollars were too expensive. Jenna now had the rough equivalent of fifteen old west dollars, which should be enough.

When she went to pay the man at the counter, he said, "There's a regular run on 1800s coins lately."

"Oh, was my friend, Sarah, here last Saturday?"

"No, I'm closed on Saturdays. It was a man, late twenties, early thirties. Don't know his name. He's been in a few times. Always buys a few dollars worth."

"Oh," said Jenna, the wheels turning in her head. Putting this news together with the cow pies she saw on that other trail—she was sure it all meant something. She just didn't know what.

CHAPTER SIXTEEN

ALTHOUGH SARAH HAD taken half a day off, it took her until two o'clock to get everything ready to go and to show up at Jenna's. That didn't surprise Jenna at all. And when Sarah brought in the stuffed-full bag, that didn't surprise Jenna, either. Then Sarah insisted on trying everything on again to make sure she had chosen the right dresses for Saturday night and especially her debut on Friday night.

When Sarah dragged out the fifth dress, Jenna said, "You're taking five dresses for a two-night engagement?"

"No, of course not. Only four. One for each night that I sing, one to ride over, and one to ride back."

"Oh, naturally," said Jenna. Her friend tried her patience at times, but Sarah had a good heart. Jenna smiled and asked, "Are we ready to go yet?"

"Have we decided which dress I'm going to leave behind?"

"I thought we decided you'd leave the pink one behind."

"Oh, that's right. I'm a little scatterbrained right now. All I can think about is singing tonight and if I chose the correct songs. You said the sheriff didn't recognize 'Home on the Range,' and it was written in 1873. So I only chose songs written before then."

"I'm sure that will be fine, Sarah." Jenna tried not to let her impatience show.

As Sarah carefully packed the four chosen dresses into the bag, she said, "I've been thinking about what you said, about how he's happily married."

Jenna knew that she meant Marcus, her boss. So she said, "Mmhmmm."

"So, I decided to let him go—in my mind, that is. I've been imagining him with food stains all over his ties and expensive shirts!"

"That's a good one!" said Jenna.

"And I've been imagining him—with her. That one is more difficult, though. Mostly, I try not to think of him. Whenever he popped into my mind this week, I thought about singing at the saloon instead. Worked every time!"

"That's great! Are we ready yet, Sarah?" asked Jenna, as she walked to the door carrying her own bag.

"Oh, wow, yes. How did it get this late?"

CHAPTER SEVENTEEN

JOSIAH HAD NO idea what it was. Well, no, that's not true. It was a cigarette, or a stub of a cigarette, but he'd never seen anything in his life quite like it. It was the fattest, most perfect cigarette he had ever seen; and it didn't look hand rolled. Although there was tobacco on the burned end, there was something strange stuck on the end of it. And the paper covering the cigarette was white with brown over the strange thing on the end. There was even printing on it! Right next to the brown part of the paper. It said, "Marlboro Lights." What did that mean?

Well, his search was successful, even if he had no idea what to do with the information. His first stop was to find the rancher. Now that it was later in the afternoon, he should find him back at the ranch house or in the barn doing the afternoon milking. But the ranch house was the opposite direction from home. Would he make it back in time for supper with Jenna? He didn't know if he would or not. He had a job to do. Right now, that had to be his focus. Although thoughts of Jenna kept threatening to intrude.

Josiah found the rancher in the barn, an old guy with

graying hair and a stubborn and crabby demeanor. While the old guy finished milking the cow, he told him what he had found.

"Naw, I've never seen or heard of such a thing," said the old man. "What makes you think it's a clue?"

There was a reason none of these guys were the sheriff, thought Josiah. "Because it doesn't belong there. Here, look at it." Josiah waited while the old guy straightened up and stretched his back.

"This ranching business is getting harder and harder the older I get. Give it to me."

Josiah handed it to the man and waited. The old guy turned it around and around in his fingers. He tried to look through it from one end to the other. "It looks like a cigarette, but what's this thing on the end of it? Maybe it's a stopper of some sort. No, it's not mine. I've never seen anything like it."

All Josiah needed was a confirmation that it didn't belong to the rancher. Now that he had it, he needed to get on his way. "All right," he opened his hand toward the rancher, "I'll let you know if I find out anything. I'd like it back, though, so I can continue my investigation."

"I don't know how this thing is going to help you, Sheriff. You found it on my property, so by all rights it's mine." He looked at the sheriff defiantly and held the cigarette in his hand as if to keep it from Josiah. Then he relented and dropped it into Josiah's palm. "But, I guess I don't need it for anything. There ya go."

"Thanks," said Josiah, ignoring the rancher's rudeness. "I am hoping that this will help me find the culprit." Josiah put the cigarette back into his shirt pocket and climbed into the saddle. "Good-bye." He was headed away from the ranch before he heard the rancher's reply.

If the old guy made one.

It took him twice as long as he had intended at the big ranch because of stopping to see the crabby old rancher. Now he had to decide if he would take the time to stop and get his new shirt. No question. He had to have that shirt. This was his first personal meeting with Jenna—instead of running into her in town—and he wanted to make a good impression.

An extra hour later, he had stopped, picked up and paid for his shirt—a good deal at a dollar and two bits—and now was on his way back to town. He would be late. No question about that now. How late was the question. After another hard week of riding, he wasn't going to hurry Patches. But, if Patches was eager to get home and started to trot to get there, Josiah wouldn't stop him.

CHAPTER EIGHTEEN

AT FOUR O'CLOCK, Jenna and Sarah walked out to the barn. They saddled their horses, tied their bags to the back of the saddles, and were off.

On their way, Jenna told Sarah about the fence marks and cow pies at the end of the cutoff trail. Then she told her about what the coin guy had said.

"You have to tell him!" said Sarah.

"Tell who?"

"Your boy, that's who! Sheriff what's-his-name!"

"Tell him what, Sarah? The cow pies and the old coins are meaningless without some context. Are cows missing? As of right now, I haven't heard anything like that. Besides, then I'd have to tell him 'when' I'm from. I'm not ready to do that. Maybe never on that one."

"What if you get involved with him? Then what? You won't tell him *when* you're from then?"

"Right now, it's harmless flirtation. And most likely it will stay that way. The idea of becoming involved with a cowboy from a hundred years ago is ridiculous."

"So is finding a portal to another time."

"Yes, that much is true."

"Are you open to getting involved with him—if it happens?" asked Sarah.

"I can't think about that now. All I know is that he's the first guy that I've liked—at all—since Daniel dumped me."

"Ouch. Don't say it like that."

"How else should I say it? That's what happened."

"Yes, but he was a jerk. You should have dumped him! Even your grandmother didn't like him, and she likes everybody."

"Well, Granny doesn't really like everybody, but she definitely took an instant and strong dislike for Daniel."

"Here's the cave. Are you ready for the old west?"

"Let's go for it!" said Jenna.

Not long after, they were in front of the hotel dismounting from their horses. They untied their bags from their saddles and walked into the hotel. This time, Jenna didn't make Jet stay with the horses. She held the door open to let Jet follow her in.

"Hi, Eliza!" said Jenna when she saw the woman behind the counter. "I'd like you to meet my dog, Jet, and my friend, Sarah, who is going to sing at the saloon the next two nights."

"I like how you introduce your dog, first," Sarah huffed playfully.

"Priorities," said Jenna.

"Nice to meet you, Sarah," said Eliza as she came out from behind the counter and walked toward Jet. "And nice to meet you, too, Jet!" Jet held her paw out, which delighted Eliza. "Oh, what a sweetheart she is."

When Eliza returned behind the counter, Sarah said, "I need a room for two nights. If you have one with two beds, Jen and I can share it."

73

Eliza looked at Jenna for confirmation. When Jenna nodded, Eliza said, "I think we have just the room for you, number twenty-four, on the second floor."

"Oh, can we have one on the first floor?" asked Sarah.

Eliza smiled. "All our hotel rooms are on the second floor, Sarah."

"Oh, fine then. Twenty-four sounds perfect. How much is it?"

"Two dollars."

Sarah dug inside her plain, leather purse trying to find the coins that had fallen to the bottom. "For each night?"

"For both nights!"

"Great deal!" said Sarah as she handed Eliza four half dollars.

"Thank you! Yours is the third room to the right," said Eliza.

Sarah and Jenna walked up the staircase, with Jet following. Sarah opened the door, took a step inside, and gasped. "Oh, dear. What did we get ourselves into?"

"What's wrong with it?" Jenna whispered as she pushed past Sarah. It was a plain room with one window. Worn rugs covered the floor. She saw two narrow beds and a wooden "sink" that had a ceramic bowl placed inside it. The bowl had water in it, and a pitcher of water sat on the sink next to the bowl. There was one kerosene lamp on the wall by the door. A chamber pot was in one corner and a small wood stove, with a stack of wood next to it, was in another corner.

One feature of the room was amazing, though. There were beautiful oil paintings on the walls. One painting showed two cowboys branding a calf, and the other showed a lake surrounded by trees. A bird with something clutched in its talons was flying away from the main scene.

Jenna looked around and whispered, "There's no bathroom."

Sarah closed the door to the room. "Oh, sorry, I forgot to tell you. When you went to see Eliza last week, I had to use the bathroom. It was an outhouse behind the saloon. Can you imagine trying to pee while holding this up?" She held up her long, flowing dress. "It was awful! I'm lucky I didn't wet myself! This should give you second thoughts about falling in love with your sheriff man."

"He's not *my* sheriff man, Sarah, and maybe it should give you second thoughts about singing in a saloon here."

"Okay, we're even. I'll take this bed." She put her bag on the bed and began unpacking. Taking the first dress out, she looked around the room. "Where's the closet?"

"No closet," said Jenna.

"Then where are the hangers?" Sarah looked hurt.

"Calm, Sarah, calm. There are these." Jenna pointed to several large pegs nailed to one wall. "Hang your stuff on these. That's what the cowboys do!"

Jenna put her one dress on a peg and sat down on the bed. "I think it's homey. I like it here."

Sarah undressed, put on a dress from her bag, and then hung up the other three on the pegs. "It will do. I'm going to go sing! That will make me feel better! See ya later, Jenna! I hope you enjoy your dinner with mister sheriff man," said Sarah, as she bounced out the door and down the stairs.

CHAPTER NINETEEN

JENNA DIDN'T KNOW what time supper was, so she decided she should change clothes now. She hung her riding dress on the peg and put the other one on. Then she walked downstairs to talk to Eliza.

"Hi, Jenna! Is the room comfortable for you?"

"Yes, it's fine, Eliza. Can I do something to help you with dinner?"

"No, no, child, you're a guest. After I've known you awhile, I'll drag you in to help me. Tonight, though, you're a guest!"

"I don't have to be a guest. I'd be happy to help."

"No, but thank you for offering, Jenna. Oh, here comes Mary Elizabeth. Let me introduce you." Eliza watched as the young woman came down the stairs. "Mary Elizabeth, I'd like you to meet Jenna, she's new to town, too. I think."

Jenna shrugged her shoulders and said, "Nice to meet you, Mary Elizabeth." She could tell the woman wore a tight corset. Jenna thought she could encircle the woman's waist with one hand. And she had huge boobs. Ah, this woman Ryan would love! I wonder why Josiah didn't go after her? Or maybe he did . . .

"Nice to meet you, Jenna," said Mary Elizabeth as she did a slight curtsy. Then she continued walking and stepped out the front door.

"Jenna," said Eliza, "we won't be ready to eat for an hour. You should go watch your friend sing."

Jenna looked around the room and noticed all the oil paintings on the wall—similar to the ones in her room. "These paintings are beautiful, Eliza. Who paints them?"

"My father used to paint all the time, but oil paints are hard to come by these days. Even Henry—you know, he runs the general store—can't seem to order them. Dad did do a great job, didn't he?"

"He's talented!" said Jenna.

"I better get back to the kitchen now, Jenna. You run along."

Jenna smiled and walked out the door. Oh! She had forgotten about their horses. They couldn't stay in front of the hotel, and they needed food and water. Old west towns must have a place for horses. She ducked back into the hotel door.

"Eliza? Is there a place I can keep our horses?"

Eliza rushed out from the back room. "Yes, dear, go left out the door and then turn right at the corner. The livery stable is right down the street."

"Thanks!" said Jenna and stepped back out the door. She walked to the black horse and stroked his face. "I'm sorry, Magic. How could I forget about you?" Looking into his liquid brown eyes, she kissed him on the nose. "Let's go."

Following Eliza's directions, she led the horses down the street. She turned the corner and a minute later saw the livery stable. Livery stable! How could she forget it was called a livery stable!

It was a large brick building with "Livery Stable" painted above the wide door. She stepped inside and inhaled deeply of the mixture of aromas including leather tack, hay, and horse manure. They were such familiar, comforting smells that she forgot for a minute that she was a hundred or more years in the past. That wonderful smell of horses never changed. And she was grateful for that.

A tall, lanky man appeared from the back and walked briskly toward her. "Can I help you, ma'am?"

"Yes, sir, can I board these two horses here?"

"You sure can, ma'am! For how long?"

"This one," she nodded toward Sarah's horse, "for two days. The black one probably just one." Probably? Why did she say that? She was going home tomorrow, wasn't she? Was she? She had a feeling she wasn't.

"Two bits a day for the two horses. We'll give them a good rub-down today; it looks like they've been traveling. Hay and water of course. Any special treatment?"

"No grain," said Jenna.

"Are you sure, ma'am? It's not any extra."

"No, I'm sure." Jenna started digging in her purse for the money, but looked up when the man spoke.

"You can pay when you pick up the horses."

"Okay, thank you very much. My name is Jenna Leyton."

"Yes, ma'am, Mrs. Leyton. We'll take good care of your horses."

Jenna thought about correcting him, but she wasn't fond of "Miss," and he would have no idea what she meant if she said, "Ms." So, she smiled and left the building.

She walked back the way she had come and pushed through the swinging doors into the saloon. Sarah was belting out "Oh, Shenandoah" and doing a beautiful job. Her singing really was lovely. There were only a few people in there, but they all clapped. Matthew behind the bar clapping the loudest, Jenna noticed. Next Sarah sang a song that Jenna didn't recognize. She did her homework, thought Jenna. When Sarah finished, Jenna walked across the room, put a quarter into Sarah's tip jar, and smiled at her friend. Then she walked back across the street. It was almost time for supper, and she was getting nervous.

As she walked across the street, she wondered why it was so wide. It was much wider than any "normal" street in her time. She walked into the hotel and heard Eliza call from the back, "Jenna, is that you? Come into the back here."

Jenna walked into the sitting room and saw the table was all set. For four. But there was no sign of Josiah. She wondered if he was the fourth, or if maybe Eliza had invited that Mary Elizabeth woman or someone else.

Jenna heard Eliza say, "Samuel, go out there, introduce yourself, and entertain our young guest."

A man walked into the room. He was slender, balding on top, but attractive. Although he smiled at her, she thought she saw a sadness behind his eyes. She wondered why.

"Hallo, Miss Jenna! I'm Samuel, Eliza's husband. Very nice to meet you." He did a slight bow.

"Nice to meet you, too, Samuel." She curtsied. "Thank you for inviting me into your home."

"Oh, that's Eliza's way, dear. She's like a mother hen."

"Well, I appreciate it. Thank you."

"Would you like to sit down, my dear?" He held out a side chair for her. Jenna sat down, and Samuel sat at the head of the table.

"So you're new to these parts, Jenna?"

"Well, yes, kind of," said Jenna, trying to be vague. "Have you lived here all your life?"

"No, Eliza and I lived most of our lives in Pennsylvania. Her parents had moved out here years ago and bought this place. But when her mother started doing poorly, they asked us to come out to help. And," he hesitated and looked away, "and Eliza wanted to get away from the war."

As Jenna was calculating in her head what year it might be, Eliza rushed in from the kitchen with a red checkered apron over her long dress.

"All done. It's keeping warm in there while we wait for our other guest. I wonder what's keeping him. He's usually not late like this."

"Josiah had to go out to that ranch today. Maybe something delayed him," said Samuel.

"That's right," said Eliza. "Well, we won't wait for him too long." Eliza looked out the window and turned to Jenna. "So how was your day today, Jenna?"

"It was mostly getting ready to come over here." After she said it, she thought she might have opened a door she didn't want to open.

Eliza said, "Oh, look, there's our brave sheriff now." She looked out the window and waved. "He should be here in a few minutes. He's going to drop off his horse."

Jenna looked out and saw Josiah riding by on his horse, with his dog trailing behind—just like her, Magic, and Jet. That reminded her about Jet. She looked around for her dog. Jet usually followed so close behind, Jenna

80

didn't have to worry about her. But she hadn't noticed her since she came into the hotel. There she was. Lying close to Eliza's old dog. Jenna looked out the window again and saw that Josiah had already disappeared.

While they waited for Josiah, the conversation turned into small talk, which pleased Jenna. She was excited to see Josiah again. He looked very handsome on that horse. She felt her heart speed up which made her uncomfortable. Was she letting herself get hurt again falling for a man from another *century?*

Then Eliza suddenly stood up and asked Jenna to help her in the kitchen. It surprised Jenna, because before Eliza had been insistent that she didn't want help.

"I'll be glad to help you, Eliza, so our guest doesn't have to," said Samuel.

"No, you stay seated, Samuel. Jenna offered to help. We women will be fine! Right, Jenna?"

Jenna followed the woman into the back and said, "Right!"

CHAPTER TWENTY

THE TRIP HOME took Josiah longer than he had expected. He had hoped to get back in time to clean up a little. But with as late as he was going to be, that wasn't going to happen now. Then he came to that widened deer trail that he had looked at earlier. And he was thinking that he should check it out again.

It would make him even later, but he thought it was the right thing to do. Eliza wouldn't be upset once she knew why he was late. And Jenna shouldn't be upset, either, if she knew he was doing his job. He hoped. It was too early in their acquaintance to chance doing anything to trouble her. Sometimes it was difficult being a man *and* being the sheriff. Making his decision, he turned Patches back onto the deer trail.

He looked at the ground carefully, not sure what he was even looking for. There, off to the left under that bush. It was a cow pie under a bush. In his experience, he had never seen a cow go under a bush before. He kept looking. Up ahead, another one and another. It was as if someone had brushed them aside so no one would see them.

Then he came to the mouth of the cave again. Drawing a deep breath because it was getting later and later, he guided Patches into the cave. He didn't have to go far to find more cow pies in the cave. That's all he needed to see, so he turned Patches around.

One cow might somehow manage to leave a cow pie under a low bush. Several? Definitely not. And with no fences, there was always the chance the closest rancher could have lost several of his cows wandering off and getting lost. But the ranchers on the other side of town who had also lost cows? Wasn't possible. Add that to the odd object in his pocket, and it all added up to someone stealing the cows and taking them through the cave. To where? He'd find that out tomorrow when he had more time.

He was on the trail of the rustler now; he was sure of that. What he thought would be a frustrating, futile week, had taken a fortunate turn. He looked down at the dog walking beside his horse. "I owe this to you, Bingo!" The dog looked up at the rider and wagged his tail. "I wouldn't have seen that strange cigarette if it hadn't been for you sniffing it out for me. Thank you!"

Closer to town now, Patches started walking faster. Josiah didn't stop him. He was eager to get to town and to share with Samuel what he had found. Could he do that in front of Jenna? Surely she wasn't the rustler. The cattle had been disappearing months before she had even shown up. No, it wasn't her. She was safe. She was also beautiful, he thought. And that thought made him smile.

Josiah sighed. Town. Finally. Patches had started to trot when they were close. Now as he rode past the hotel window, he saw Eliza wave to him. He'd hoped that she'd see him so she knew he was on his way. Eliza and

Samuel were like parents to him. He didn't like to keep them waiting. Patches turned the corner and approached the livery stable.

Josiah called out as he rode into the big brick building. "Ezra! Ezra!" He hoped Ezra was around. If he had to take care of Patches himself, it would delay him even longer.

Ezra walked quickly up to Josiah. "Sorry, Sheriff. Just in the back eating my supper."

"No need to apologize, Ezra. I'm in a hurry, so I am glad you're here. Can you take care of Patches for me?"

"Yes, sure, first thing!"

Josiah smiled at the man. "No need to take care of him before your supper, Ezra. Take your time. Patches'll wait. Thanks!"

Josiah swung off Patches and walked briskly toward the hotel, with Bingo following. He couldn't help himself; he smiled with anticipation at seeing the woman again. Maybe he'd find out more about her this evening, so she wouldn't be such a mystery to him. Although maybe the mystery *is* what he liked about her.

He walked into the hotel, careful not to act like "a cowboy just off the range" as Eliza put it. Walking into the sitting room, he turned to see Samuel sitting at the table alone, so his smile drooped.

"Not happy to see me, Josiah?" asked Samuel.

"Yes, of course, Samuel. I, I—"

"No need to finish, youngster, I understand! I was young once, too."

Josiah smiled and sat by the window. He looked expectantly at Samuel.

"Don't worry, son, she'll be right out. She's helping Eliza in the kitchen right now. So, did you find anything today or was it another useless trip?"

Josiah was about to tell Samuel what he had found, when Jenna came out of the back room carrying a platter of baked chicken. An audible gasp escaped him as he struggled to stand. She had a different dress on and looked beautiful.

CHAPTER TWENTY-ONE

JENNA HEARD JOSIAH'S gasp and thought she understood why Eliza asked her to help in the kitchen. She glanced back toward Eliza. When the older woman winked, she knew she was right. Eliza had wanted Josiah to get the whole image of Jenna walking into the room.

As she walked toward the table, Jenna said, "Hallo, Josiah. Good to see you again." While the tongue-tied Josiah tried to find something to say, Jenna turned around to Eliza and said, "Can I help you with anything else, Eliza?"

"No, dear," said Eliza. "Just sit down and visit."

"Hallo, Jenna," Josiah finally said. "How have you been? Did you have a good week?"

"Yes, how about you?"

"It was a tough week, but I'm glad to be here now."

"Have you always lived in Red Bluff, Josiah?"

"No, I grew up back East," said Josiah.

"The boy is Boston born and raised," added Samuel.

"Boston? Really? Why did you leave?" asked Jenna.

"I was in college to become a lawyer, like my parents wanted, but I knew that life wasn't for me. As far back as

I could remember, I wanted to come out west."

Eliza sat down and began passing the food around the table. The chicken was baked with stewed tomatoes, and there was also some boiled cabbage. Jenna noticed there wasn't any salad. Then she realized there wouldn't be this time of year until people could start their gardens. Eliza would have canned the tomatoes and kept the cabbage in a root cellar.

While everyone was busy taking their food, she thought about what Josiah had said. She had underestimated Josiah—she thought he was just a dumb hick. A pretty boy, but a dumb hick. His next statement confirmed her mistake.

When everyone finished taking their portions, Josiah exhaled and said, "My parents were furious with me because I was doing so well in my classes. But it just wasn't me. I don't think they've forgiven me yet for coming out west and not joining the family practice."

"Your father is an attorney, then, too?" asked Jenna, discomfited because of her mistake.

Josiah nodded his head and took another bite of chicken. "But I've never regretted coming out here. Not for one minute. And my adoptive parents," he looked at Samuel and Eliza and smiled, "are glad I'm here."

"Yes, we are," said Samuel. "You wouldn't have believed this town before Josiah here came out and straightened everything up. Gunfights and killings every day. Everyone afraid. It was awful."

"Samuel, Jenna is the young woman who witnessed the gunfight a couple of weeks ago when Josiah was out of town," said Eliza.

"Oh, that's right," said Samuel. "So you can imagine what it was like before Josiah."

"Josiah had some unusual ways of handling the gun-fighting situation, but they worked," said Eliza with a loving smile toward Josiah.

"I think I got lucky," said Josiah.

"Josiah, you were about to tell me if today's ride was worth it or not. Did you find anything or was it a waste?" asked Samuel.

"Well, I did discover a couple of interesting things," said Josiah. "There was a path off the main trail that looked like a wide deer trail. When I followed it, I found the strangest thing. Someone had pushed the cow pies under bushes, as if to hide them. It wasn't just one or two, it was several. And there were no cow tracks, just the cow pies."

Jenna held her breath while Josiah took two more bites of chicken. Had he discovered the cave? And what if he had? What would that mean? Then Josiah continued.

"Maybe one cow could get in a strange enough position for a cow pie to land under a bush, but definitely not several." Suddenly he looked up. "Oh, Eliza? I'm sorry to be talking about this at the dinner table."

"No need to be sorry, my boy. Nobody here is so particular to object to a few cow pies!" Eliza smiled. "But it reminds me about dessert! Does anyone want second helpings, or can I get the apple pie?"

"Eliza, this was so delicious. Can I help you clear the table?"

"No, my dear. You're company. You stay right here and enjoy the men's company." She looked at Josiah, but he didn't notice. "I'll be right back."

Eliza took her plate, Jenna's plate, and the almost empty platter of chicken into the back. Jenna watched her as she walked away. When she stood up to help,

Samuel put his hand on hers.

"No, Jenna dear, let her do it. Eliza wants you to stay here."

Jenna sat back down again, as Josiah resumed his story. She thought he looked so handsome talking so enthusiastically about his work.

"Let me show you something while Eliza is in the other room. Cow pies are one thing, but she wouldn't want this out at the dinner table!" Josiah reached into his shirt pocket and pulled out the cigarette. "What do you make of it, Samuel?"

Samuel took the object from Josiah and turned it around in his fingers. "I have no idea, Jos. I can't recollect ever seeing anything like this. It's like a cigarette, but it's so perfect. And this printing on it—very strange."

"That's what I thought, too, Samuel." He turned his head as he heard Eliza returning, so he reached out to take the cigarette back from Samuel and drop it into his pocket. As Eliza approached the table with the delicious smelling apple pie, Josiah said, "Oh, no!"

"What's wrong, Josiah?" asked Eliza as she set the pie on the table and grabbed his and Samuel's plates and the rest of the cabbage.

"Oh, my shirt! My new shirt! I forgot to put it on!" Then he looked at Jenna sheepishly. She kept her eyes on the pie and pretended not to notice his discomfort.

Eliza started to return the leftover food and dirty plates to the kitchen, when she said, "That's a shame, Josiah." She turned around to look at Jenna. "I think we need to do this again tomorrow night, so Josiah can show off his new shirt. Are you willing to come back and eat supper with us again tomorrow?"

"Oh, no, Eliza. Thank you for asking, but I couldn't

possibly impose on you like that!"

"Jenna, you can stay in Sarah's room again—she'll be here another night, won't she?" Jenna nodded. "And it's no imposition at all. We have to eat, don't we? All right. It's settled then," and she turned around and stepped into the kitchen.

A minute later she returned with several small plates and a knife to cut the pie. She cut the pie and doled out the pieces to everyone. "So, what was that you showed to Samuel that you didn't want me to see?" asked Eliza.

"You heard? Oh, sorry, Eliza," said Josiah.

"Well, what was it then? You're not going to get off scot-free, Josiah. You have to show me!"

"Aw, Eliza," said Josiah.

"Come on, boy, come on," said Eliza.

Josiah reached into his shirt pocket and handed the cigarette to Eliza. "Here it is."

"So, why would you keep this from me?"

"I know how you hate cigarettes."

"It's the smoke, Josiah. I can't stand the smoke. But this, this isn't a cigarette."

Josiah looked confused. "Then what is it?"

Eliza looked up and smiled. "It's a clue! Here, look at this, Jenna. Have you ever seen anything like it? Look at the printing there. It says Marlboro Lights. What do you suppose that means?"

Jenna didn't need a closer look to know exactly what it was. She looked at the cigarette but didn't take it from Eliza. Then she innocently shrugged her shoulders. Trying not to sound too obvious, she said, "This pie is delicious, Eliza!" It was. Home made and pure ingredients. Nothing better.

Eliza handed the cigarette back to Josiah. "Well, what

are you going to do with that clue, Josiah?"

"Well, I don't rightly know. Maybe show it around town and see if it sparks any interest. See if anybody knows what it is."

The conversation quieted while everyone enjoyed their pie. When Eliza finished her last mouthful, she said, "How about a walk after dinner?"

Jenna, thinking she could spend more time with Josiah, quickly agreed. Josiah agreed, also. And Jenna hoped that was because he wanted to spend more time with her. Samuel thought the walk was a good idea, too.

When everyone stood up and headed toward the door, Eliza said, "You know, I'm a little tired. I think I'll stay here and clean up."

Immediately, Jenna said, "I'll stay to help."

"You will not, Jenna. You're my guest. You go on and walk with Josiah. Samuel?"

Samuel looked at her without understanding. But when Jenna saw Eliza glance at her and Josiah, he figured it out. "Oh, yes, I will stay to help Eliza. You two run along."

"Thank you so much for dinner, Eliza. Everything was wonderful," said Jenna.

"I'll see you for dinner tomorrow, child, remember?"

"Yes, Eliza, I remember. Thank you."

Josiah hesitated so Jenna could walk out the door first. When they reached the front door of the hotel, Josiah held the door open for Jenna. And Jenna thought how wonderful it was to be with an old-fashioned man who held doors open for her. Except he wasn't old-fashioned. This was his time.

CHAPTER TWENTY-TWO

"How about if I show you around town?" asked Josiah.

"That would be great, Josiah."

Outside the hotel, they turned left and walked down the street. The two dogs, Jet and Bingo, followed companionably behind them.

"So, where are you from, exactly?"

"Um, well, that's a difficult question. Kind of from here. Kind of."

"That's what you told me last time I asked. You are a mystery, aren't you?" He smiled.

"Josiah, when I get to know you better, well, if, then you'll know more," Jenna said.

He stopped walking, turned toward her, and said, "Yes, I'd like to get to know you better." But the moment must have made him uncomfortable, because then he faced forward again and motioned to the school on the corner. "This is our school. We painted it last fall."

"Who painted it?" asked Jenna.

"Most of the town helped. That's how jobs usually get done around here."

"That's cool. I miss that."

"It's not like that in your town—wherever that is?"

"Not anymore," said Jenna. "Is it a one-room school-house?"

"Yes, it is. Would you like to see it?"

"I'd love to!"

They crossed the street and walked to the door. Josiah opened it.

"It's not locked?"

"Why should it be locked?" asked Josiah.

"How things have changed." Jenna shook her head.

Inside, it was an amazing place. There was a chalk-board up at the front, a teacher's desk and chair, and benches lined up from the front to the back of the room.

"Where are the student's desks?"

"What do you mean?"

"What do they write on?"

"They have slates and chalk. It works fine."

Jenna thought she'd like to get them desks. She sur-prised herself with that thought, because it made her think that she was beginning to think of this place as home. It already was, in a way. She grew up in Red Bluff. And this was Red Bluff.

"Thanks for showing me, Josiah."

They walked across the wide street toward the livery stable. "On this side of the street, is Doc's office," said Josiah.

"Has Doc gone to college?"

"Yes, of course! Don't doctors go to college where you're from?"

"Yes, definitely. For many years."

"Now that you mention it, though, I think Doc told me that he apprenticed before college and that some doctors never go to school." When Jenna nodded, he

93

continued. "Ah, here we are at the livery stable. Your horse is probably in there already, right?"

"Yes, he is. My horse and Sarah's horse. What's that fella's name who takes care of the horses?"

"The young one?" Jenna nodded. "That's Ezra. His father, Frank, is usually in the blacksmith's shop next door." They walked a little farther. "Here is the feed store. It's usually a busy place. And next to that is the post office and then the firehouse."

They turned the corner and kept walking. They crossed the street again and were on the same block as the hotel.

"Josiah, why are the streets so wide? It seems like overkill."

"Overkill? What's overkill?"

"Oh, sorry. Um, too wide—more wide than necessary."

"No, it's the perfect width. Just big enough for a large wagon pulled by a team of horses to turn around."

"Oh! That makes perfect sense."

Josiah nodded. "Right now, we're standing in front of the stage line office. The telegraph office shares the building. They have a small room at the front. And across the street, you see our general store, my office, and the bank."

"The jail is right there with your office?"

"Yes. I sleep there, too. That way, someone is always around to keep an eye on the bad guys!"

"How long have you been sheriff?"

"A little more than two years."

"Did you ever catch any bank robbers?"

Josiah nodded shyly. "Twice. Both times I got lucky."

Jenna looked at him expectantly, but he remained

quiet. "Go ahead. I want to hear the story!"

"The first one isn't a story that you tell in front of a lady."

Jenna, thinking back to the first time he saw her, said, "Try me. I'm tough. Remember, I sometimes wear men's clothing!"

That perked Josiah up—he wanted to ask about her pants. But, instead, he began the first story.

"I had eaten something bad. Really bad. So I was in the necessary and had been for half an hour, at least. Some cowboys were standing behind it, planning a robbery. They didn't know I was in there, and they talked about where they would meet afterward to split the money. I missed the robbery itself because I was still stuck in the necessary. But afterward, I knew exactly where to find them." He didn't look her in the eye until he finished the story. Then he said, "And the rest was easy."

Jenna clapped her hands. She didn't know what a "necessary" was, but from the context, she figured he meant the outhouse. "That was a great story! What about the other one?"

"The other one happened before the outhouse incident and was another lucky accident. I had just become sheriff and hadn't been in town too long. This was before my friendship with Eliza and Samuel. When I woke up in the middle of the night feeling lonely, I couldn't go back to sleep. There was a full moon out, so I decided to go walking around town. My first thought was to go visit Patches. You have a horse. You know how it is. You may not have a friend in the world, but if you have your horse, you're okay.

"As I returned from there, the back way, I saw some-

95

one coming out the back door of the bank. He didn't see me because I was in the shadows. But I thought it was strange. Although he had something pulled over his head, I recognized him as the bank president. When I got close enough, I spoke to him thinking maybe he needed help with something. He was so scared, he dropped the saddlebags he carried. When I picked them up, some money dropped out. So I knew what was going on.

"After that, the townsfolk had more respect for me and accepted me. At first when I got here and got the job, they weren't sure that an eastern boy could do the job. When this happened, they started looking at me differently."

"Another great story, Josiah!"

"Come on, let's cross the street." He held out his arm for her, and she slid hers into it as natural as could be. Natural except that her heart fluttered uncontrollably.

When they reached the other side of the street, she noticed the general store was still open. "Josiah, come into the store with me. I want to see what they sell."

"It's the same as any other general store, Jenna. Don't they have stores where you live?"

"Yes, but this one is different. Come on. Come in with me."

Josiah patted her arm and removed his. "I can't go in there right now. Not at closing time. You can go tomorrow. Now isn't a good time."

"Oh, come on. I'll just be a few minutes."

"No, Jenna. I'm going back to my office. Come in when you're finished."

"Okay, I'll see you in a few minutes."

Josiah turned toward his office and said under his

breath, "More like a few hours."

Jenna only half heard him and had no idea what he meant, anyway. She wondered if she had said something wrong. He left her so abruptly. No use worrying about it now. She'd just take a quick peek in the store and then join him in his office.

CHAPTER TWENTY-THREE

JENNA WALKED THROUGH the door and said hello to the owner. That was the second to the last word she uttered while she was there.

"Hallo, ma'am. I'm Henry Ralston. You must be that new woman everybody is talking about." Jenna thought, everybody is talking about me? But before she could answer, Henry continued as if reading her thoughts. "Yes, yes, of course they're talking about you. It's a small town. They'll talk about anything they can.

"So where are you from?" he asked Jenna. Again not waiting for her to answer, he went on. "Yes, yes. Me? I'm not from here, either. Arrived on the stage with almost nothing, and look how I built this place up. It was nothing when I first started working here, and look at her now! There used to be no selection in this place! Since I've taken over, I've expanded more and more. I'm happy to say that my store rivals any in the big city!

"You came on horseback? Not me. No, no. As I said, I arrived on the stage. I've never needed a horse. Seems like an unnecessary expense and responsibility. If I need to get anywhere, I'll rent a team and wagon. Then I return them, and I'm finished. I don't have to worry about feeding them or taking care of them or worrying about them. I just return the team, and I'm done.

"Did I tell you the store is for sale? Yes, yes. And whoever buys it will buy a thriving business now. A thriving business, I tell you. Not like when I bought it. No, no. This place is making oodles of money. The man who buys this will be a lucky man! I don't even know why I want to sell, I'm making so much money. But some things are more important, you know? And I'd like to return to the big city from whence I came. I won't ride a horse out of here, either. No, no. I will ride in the stagecoach, first class. So if you know of anyone who wants to buy this store, send them my way."

Jenna finally tuned him out. At first, she marveled at how he could go on and on without catching his breath. And how he could go so smoothly from one subject to the next without even a pause. But the novelty had worn off, and now she just wanted to look around.

Ignoring him, she looked around the store. There were shelves, crates, and barrels haphazardly placed everywhere. You could not walk from one side of the store to the other in a straight line. Different items were crammed and jammed everywhere. The store was a reflection of Henry Ralston. He was jammed with words, and the store was jammed with *stuff*.

There was a stack of four or five buckets on the floor. In the top bucket were some socks, a pistol, and a handful of bullets. A long length of rope hung on the wall behind the buckets. She stepped farther into the store and saw a shelf with lanterns, pots and pans, and some random dishes. Across from her stood several bolts of cloth. On the other side of the store she saw food items like sacks of flour, sugar, and dried beans. Farther over, she saw some canned vegetables.

As Henry's voice droned on, she stepped back toward the door. Stealing a quick glance toward his voice, she noticed a cash register on the counter. On one side of it was a coffee grinder, and on the other side was a scale. She had seen enough. Nodding her head toward Henry, she said, "Good-bye" and scurried out the door.

She took a deep breath and leaned against the closed door. Then, in a moment of panic, she thought that if he saw her by the door he might come out and continue talking, so she moved in front of the building where he couldn't see her from the inside.

Her heart beat fast, and she took another deep breath. This wasn't the same quick heart beat she felt when she was with Josiah. This was something that felt like she had just escaped. Yes, that was it. Escaped from an assault of words. She felt like she had barely escaped with her life. Then she started laughing at the absurdity of it all, and she couldn't stop.

CHAPTER TWENTY-FOUR

JOSIAH WALKED INTO his office and sat down in a huff. Everything was going so well, why did she have to insist on going to the general store? Going in there around closing time was like asking to be assaulted with words—Henry's only weapon, words—but they were deadly. Or at least they felt that way. You walk in there, and the deluge begins and doesn't end until you can manage to escape. It leaves you gasping for air by the time you get out the door.

And *she* was in there now instead of spending time with him. He didn't know if he should feel angry or depressed. What surprised him was that he felt neither. He felt lonely. Lonely without her. Lonely for a woman whom he had never seen before two weeks earlier.

Shuffling the papers around on his desk, he thought he'd been doing a lot of that since meeting Jenna. Since that chance meeting, he couldn't get the woman out of his thoughts. He couldn't concentrate on his job. Thoughts of her invaded everything he did. Never in his life had he felt this way about a woman.

He didn't want to think that way. It was dangerous to

think that way. There was still a huge unknown with Jenna. She had never said she was going to stay here in town, and she wouldn't even tell him where she was from. Was it her aura of mystery that enchanted him so? The only way he would get an answer to that question was when he knew her better. All he knew now was that he liked everything about her. It didn't hurt that she was beautiful as well.

Josiah heard his door open and smiled when he saw Jenna and her dog coming through the door. But his smile faded when he saw her face. She was flushed and out of breath. She looked like a woman who had been— kissed. Had Henry Ralston kissed his girl before he even had a chance to?

These thoughts raced around in his head until she plunked down in the seat by his desk. "Oh, Josiah, why didn't you warn me?" Josiah's fists balled up. If that Henry kissed her without her permission, he would— Jenna interrupted his thoughts by saying, "He wouldn't shut up! And he talks so fast! You can't get a word in edgewise!"

Josiah relaxed his fists and his smile returned. "It feels like being assaulted, doesn't it?"

"Yes!" said Jenna. "That's the exact word that I used! Why didn't you warn me?"

Josiah patted her hand with his. And left his hand on top of hers. The thought of that kiss still played on his mind. "I did warn you, Jenna. I told you it was a bad time to go in there. During the day, he's chatty, but always busy measuring or figuring something. But this time in the evening, he's—well—you experienced it. There's nothing quite like it, is there?"

"No, it was awful." She took a deep breath. "I was

barely able to catch my breath. I'm only breathing normally now that I'm here."

Jenna smiled at him, and he felt his heart melt. He noticed that she looked at his hand sitting on top of hers, and then she looked away without moving it.

"So, this is your office. Will you show me around?"

Josiah reluctantly took his hand from hers and stood up. He put out his hand to help her up. Even if it was a brief instant, he loved touching her. He walked toward the door to the jail, but she stopped him in front of the wanted posters.

"See anyone you know?" laughed Josiah.

Jenna studied the wanted posters carefully. "There! Him!"

Surprised, Josiah said, "Really? You know him? Jesse James?"

"Well, I don't exactly know him. I've seen him. Well, kind of seen him. More like heard of him," stuttered Jenna.

"You've kind of seen him? You continue to mystify me, Jenna Leyton. Come on in here. Let me show you the jail." He led her into the room with the cells.

Jenna walked down the passageway and looked at the three identical cells. Each cell had a cot with a dirty mattress, a barred window, and a bucket in the corner.

"Ew," Jenna said. "Not a place I'd like to spend much time."

Josiah led her through the door and behind his desk. He opened another door. "And this is where I sleep."

"Josiah! This room looks almost like another cell. There's a clean covering on the mattress, a chamber pot instead of a bucket, but it's not much bigger, and there's even bars on the windows!"

103

Josiah shrugged. "Home, sweet home," he said as she walked back into the other room and sat on the chair again.

"Do you have a deputy?"

"To use your expression, Jenna, kind of."

"Why doesn't he sleep here at night so you can sleep in your own house?"

"Two reasons. This has been my house since I moved to town. The second reason is that my so called deputy is a bummer."

"Bummer? What's a bummer?"

"You know, the no-account town drunk."

"Why don't you get rid of him and hire someone else?"

"This is a small town. Applicants aren't exactly beating down my door."

"Don't you need a deputy for backup or something?"

"Luckily, I haven't needed any. What happened that first day you arrived in town, happened because I had been *out* of town. The deputy was dead drunk in the saloon. That poor kid didn't have to die—at least he didn't have to die in my town. But, you know, you do the best you can."

"I've had a wonderful evening, Josiah. But I should go see Sarah singing before I turn in for the night."

"Sorry, Jenna. I have to take you back to the hotel—back to Eliza. Then you can go where you please."

"Why would you have to do that?"

"Because it would be inappropriate to do anything else."

Jenna shook her head. "The customs here—well, it will take some getting used to."

"You talk about 'here' like it's some place entirely

different than where you're from." Josiah put both hands on the desk and turned his body all the way to face hers. "Jenna, I'm serious now. Please tell me. I know it sounds crazy, but are you from another planet or something?"

CHAPTER TWENTY-FIVE

JENNA LOOKED AT how serious he was. She realized that what she had just said made her sound alien to someone else. If there was ever any right time to tell Josiah the truth, it would be now. "No, I—" She looked into his eyes and then looked away. How do you tell someone you're from another time? It sounded easier than it was.

Jenna looked back into his eyes and said, "I promise you. If I were from another planet, I would tell you. But I'm not."

"Okay, I'll take your word for it. Let's get you back to Eliza's before she sends out a posse looking for you."

They walked slowly back to the hotel, but Jenna felt a difference. Josiah acted distant. Obviously he felt disappointed with her answer. It wasn't like he actually wanted her *to be* from another planet, it was that he wanted her to tell him where she was really from. Maybe she should have told him. She didn't want to lose him because of not telling him. But then again, she might lose him if she told him. It was a dilemma.

Josiah opened the door for her and the two dogs, and followed them inside. "Eliza," he called out, "I'm returning your guest to your care."

Eliza bustled out from the back. "Thank you, Josiah. You two had a pleasant walk, I trust?"

Jenna smiled. "Yes, a very enjoyable walk."

Josiah, still sober faced, said, "Yes, it was fine. I'll see you tomorrow. Good-bye, Eliza. Good-bye, Jenna." He walked out the door without turning around.

If Eliza noticed his stiffness, she didn't comment on it, which made Jenna glad. It would be as difficult explaining to Eliza as it would be to Josiah. She might have to stop coming here after this weekend. The thought of that made her miss Josiah.

Jenna perked up, squared her shoulders, and said, "Eliza, I'm going across the street to hear Sarah sing."

"Samuel and my father already walked over there."

"Oh, then why don't you come with me? Come on, we'll have a great time!"

"Jenna, I was hoping you would stay here and visit with me."

Jenna thought there was a hint of pleading in Eliza's voice. She couldn't say no after all Eliza had done for her. She didn't want to say no.

Jenna turned toward the sitting room and said, "Yes, of course I'll stay, Eliza. I'd be delighted to visit with you." She smiled at the older woman who looked relieved.

They sat down. Eliza asked, "Can I get you some tea, child?"

"No, thanks, Eliza. I'm fine."

Eliza patted Jenna's hand. "Thank you for staying tonight, Jenna. I feel like I can talk to you."

"I'm happy to stay, Eliza. I enjoy talking to you, too." When the older woman said nothing more, Jenna said,

"It surprised me that Josiah doesn't have a decent deputy. It seems dangerous for him not to have someone who could back him up if he needed it."

"Oh, that would probably be my fault, dear."

"Your fault? I don't understand. Josiah said that no one had applied."

"Oh, yes, someone has applied. My Samuel *begged* Josiah to make him deputy."

"Then why didn't Josiah do that?"

"Because I asked him not to."

Silence. But Jenna didn't think she should speak. She felt that Eliza had more to say.

"I asked him not to because I can't take any more loss. No more loss." Eliza covered her face with her hands and quietly wept.

Jenna put her hand on the older woman's arm. "I'm sorry, Eliza. I didn't mean to mention something that would hurt you."

Eliza took her hands from her face and wiped away her tears with a handkerchief that she pulled from her pocket. "It's all right, child. You didn't know, and it's about time that I face it. I've kept it hidden deep down inside me for too long now." She sniffled, blew her nose, and then said, "Excuse me.

"One reason I was happy to move out here was because, back in Pennsylvania, they were talking about war before it ever started. With two young sons, Brian and William, I wanted to get them out of there. I thought they'd be safe here.

"But it wasn't to be. When they heard about the war starting, they insisted on going back to Pennsylvania to fight with their cousins and friends. There was no stopping them. We argued with them and tried to get them to stay, but it was no use. They said if we didn't give our permission, they would run off anyway. Finally, we kissed them good-bye, put them on a train, and hoped for the best."

Eliza stopped and took a deep breath. Jenna thought how different from Henry this conversation was. Eliza hadn't stopped talking, but she spoke slowly, with plenty of pauses. Jenna could have spoken at any time, but she knew better than that. Eliza needed to get this out.

"The two boys, along with the others, ended up in Virginia fighting one of the first battles. And neither one survived it." She sniffled again and then continued. "Months later, we received a letter that they had both been killed in that first battle. They buried William there, but they had never found Brian's body.

"At first, I was certain that he was alive and it was just a matter of time before he'd come back home to us. Then years passed, and I finally gave up hope. There is still a part of me," she tapped her chest, "in here, that believes Brian is still alive. But even that feeling is starting to fade.

"It's not right for children to die before their parents. It's not right." She dabbed at her nose with her handkerchief and looked at Jenna. "So you see why I made Josiah promise not to hire Samuel as deputy. I couldn't take any more loss."

"I'm so sorry, Eliza. So sorry."

"And the worst part is that being deputy would probably have been good for Samuel. He hasn't been right since those two boys died. It bothered him especially bad. He still blames himself, although I've assured him there was nothing that either of us could have done to stop them. But the good part is having Josiah become part of the family." She looked at Jenna. "He really is like a son to us, and that has helped Samuel more than anything else.

"So now you know my sad story. You told me yours, and now I've told you mine. Maybe that's why it's easy to talk to you, child. We have this huge empty space in common."

"I'm so sorry, Eliza."

"It's finished now. Just like your parents are gone. None of them will be coming back now, will they?" Changing the subject abruptly, Eliza said, "So do you like our brave sheriff, Josiah?"

"I like him very much."

"Maybe you shouldn't, dear."

That made Jenna blink and sit back in her chair. "Why not? Is something wrong with him?"

"Oh, no, Josiah is as good a man as they come. But, I'll be honest with you, dear," she patted Jenna's hand, "when I first met you and found you to be a fine young woman, I thought you would be the perfect woman for Josiah."

"And now that you've gotten to know me, you don't think I would be?" Jenna asked, slightly offended.

Eliza patted her hand again and smiled. "Oh, no, dear, I still think you would be perfect for Josiah. But now that I know you, I want what's best for you, too. And I'm not sure Josiah would be. As long as he's sheriff, and knowing Josiah that will be a long time, but as long as he's sheriff, there is always the chance that he could run into some bad character that—well—I might as well just say it—that kills him."

"Oh!" said Jenna. "I never even considered that."

Eliza stood up. "I'm sorry to be the one to bring it to

your attention, dear. But I like you, and I didn't want the courtship to go any further without you knowing the possibilities.

"It's late now, Jenna. You should get to bed. Thanks so much for staying to talk to me. And thanks for being such a good listener."

"I enjoy talking to you, Eliza. And thank you for dinner. It was wonderful!" She hugged the older woman and made her way up the stairs, which were lighted by kerosene lamps.

CHAPTER TWENTY-SIX

SINCE SARAH CAME in late the night before, when Jenna awoke, she just lay there so as not to wake Sarah. She thought about what Eliza had said the night before. About the courtship. Courtship? Is that what was happening between her and Josiah? The thought scared her and made her excited all at the same time.

The other item that Eliza mentioned didn't bother her. Josiah dying. That would be easy enough to find out when she got back home. Look it up on the internet, one two three, and she'd know exactly when he died. She hoped from old age. But she would soon know. After her parents died and she quit her job, she had done some genealogy just to pass some time. So she knew where to look and the best way to find out.

Josiah's living or dying did not have the same impact on her as Eliza using the word courtship. If she knew he was going to die anytime soon, she wouldn't get any further involved. But—courtship—what was she going to do about that? Courtship. Wasn't that one step before marriage? If he was going to live a long time, then she had to decide. Could she really live out her life here, in the nineteenth century? Without toilets. Without electric lights. Without refrigeration. And on a more personal note—without Granny.

She loved that old woman. Her grandmother was her number one supporter. Could she really go without ever seeing her again? Did she have to? She could always take the cave back "home"—home to her own time, that is.

Which reminded her. What was she going to do about the cow pies and the cigarette that Josiah found? She felt sure they were connected. Well, pretty sure. Should she tell him? Maybe she should wait until she had more facts. Someone who had innocently stumbled on the place like she had could have easily dropped the cigarette. It was all so confusing—living between two different times.

As Jenna went over her options in her mind, Sarah stirred. "You awake yet, sleepyhead?" Jenna asked.

"I got in late."

"Whose fault is that?"

"Not mine! I was just singing, doing my job. Matthew kept asking me to stay. He said that it was helping business."

"Matthew kept asking, huh? Maybe after a couple of more nights, you should tell Matthew that if he paid you, you might consider staying later."

"I made lots of tips last night!"

"How much?"

"Two dollars and sixty-two cents."

"I think that's good money for this time," said Jenna.

"I'm happy with it. I'm glad that people like me enough to tip me."

"Are you ready to get up and have breakfast?" asked Jenna.

"Where are we going to get breakfast?"

113

"There's a restaurant downstairs—I just assumed—but, you're right. I don't know if they serve breakfast or not. Let's try. I'm hungry."

"If they don't, we can always go to the saloon. They have all kinds of free food over there."

The two women got dressed and walked down the stairs. Jenna saw Eliza and said, "Good morning, Eliza! Is the restaurant open this morning?"

"For you it is, dear. What would you like?" asked Eliza.

"Coffee, and do you have eggs?"

"I can whip up a couple of eggs for you. Sarah, what would you like?"

"Same for me, Eliza. Coffee and eggs sound terrific. Thank you."

Jenna and Sarah sat down in the empty restaurant. Eliza followed them in and walked into the restaurant kitchen. Several minutes later, she came back with a full tray. She unloaded the coffee cups first and then placed a plate of eggs and toast in front of each of them.

"Thank you!" the women said in unison.

"You're welcome. When you're finished, you're welcome to just leave. I'll add your breakfast to your hotel bill."

"Thank you, Eliza! I'll see you for dinner!"

Eliza turned back to look at Jenna. "I'm looking forward to it, dear." Then she turned around again and walked out.

"She really likes you," said Sarah.

"I really like her, too. She's a wonderful woman."

"She seems very motherly."

Jenna nodded her head. Neither of them had any more to say about that subject. They both knew where it was heading.

After breakfast, Jenna offered to give Sarah a tour of the town like Josiah had given her. After seeing the one-room schoolhouse and then Jenna pointing out the doctor's office, they stopped at the livery stable to see the horses. They were fine. The young man, Ezra, was in Magic's stall cleaning it and talking to Magic. That made Jenna smile. Anyone who treated her horse well was okay in her book.

When they arrived at the store, Jenna told her what had happened to her. Sarah insisted on going in, anyway. "I'm warning you, Sarah, it's an awful experience."

"I'm going. I'll be right out."

"Yeah, right."

Jenna stood outside and slowly made her way to the sheriff's office. Suddenly the door opened and a young woman walked out. A pang of jealousy stabbed at her heart. She took a deep breath and decided to go in anyway.

She walked in smiling. And when Josiah looked up, she said, "Hi, Josiah!"

He smiled at her. "Hallo, Jenna. What are you doing out and about on this fine day?"

"I've been giving Sarah the tour that you gave me yesterday. She insisted on going into the store even though I warned her!"

"It shouldn't be too bad right now. It's closing time when Henry can't keep his mouth shut."

"Oh, that's right. You told me that. So, what are you doing today?"

"Well, I had planned on following up on the cigarette and hidden cow pies. But Annie, the schoolteacher, came in to tell me she is selling her ranch. Now I have to deal with that."

115

"Are you buying your own place?"

"No. She wants to move into the house across the street from the school that's traditionally been for the schoolteacher. But since she lived on her ranch, it was rented out to my, ah, deputy. Now he's going to have to find another place to stay. Well, when she sells it, that is.

"And then, while she was here, a rancher came in and asked me to settle a dispute about a cow. It's way at the other side of town, so I can't research the other clues today. That disappoints me."

Just then, the door popped open and Sarah came in all smiles. "What a neat place that is! A little crowded, but he has a little of everything, doesn't he? Oh, hello, Josiah. How are you today?"

"I'm feeling peart, thanks, Sarah. Glad to see you escaped from the store with your life."

"Oh, it wasn't as bad as Jenna described it. Henry wasn't half bad. Of course, he was busy taking inventory of a new shipment he had received. Josiah, what's peart?"

"Oh, good! I'm feeling good!"

"Oh, cool. Shall we go, Jenna?"

"Sure, Sarah. Bye, Josiah. See you later."

"Good-bye, Jenna, Sarah."

CHAPTER TWENTY-SEVEN

JOSIAH HAD WANTED so badly to stay mad at Jenna. One look at her, and that plan failed. It wasn't just that she was beautiful. There were many beautiful women around. Something about her stirred something inside him. When he was around her, his heart felt like it was going to explode with joy. What difference did it make where she came from, anyway? She'd tell him eventually. He hoped.

He walked around the block to the livery and walked back to the stall where they kept Patches. Josiah knew he could ask Ezra to have Patches brushed and saddled for him. But he liked brushing his own horse. He hated that Patches had to stay in a stall instead of on pasture somewhere. But at least Ezra turned him out into the corral every day, so he had room to run. A little room, anyway.

Something he had often thought of popped into his mind again. Perhaps he should consider buying Annie's ranch. Patches would have pasture then, he could get some more horses, and maybe a few head of cattle. Unfortunately, that was just a dream. Without a good deputy, that was impossible to even hope for. Hell, a

117

decent deputy would do. He'd be better off with no deputy than that no-account Rawlins.

After finishing brushing and saddling Patches, he mounted up and rode out of town toward the bickering ranchers and the case of the unbranded cow. This cropped up now and again with unmarked cattle. Something he recently read about would change all that. Ranches back east had started using what they called "barbed wire"—a metal fence with barbs attached. It discouraged cattle from trying to break through fences. Eventually it would show up here, and then he would have one less headache to handle.

Josiah took a deep breath and looked around. He dearly loved riding around out here. From the birds singing, to the varmints scurrying, to the blue sky and the open spaces, he loved it all. Returning to a city like Boston was something that he would never consider. Of that much, he was sure.

Josiah rode along, silently contemplative, enjoying being outside, when thoughts of Jenna intruded on him. Dang that woman, thought Josiah. What was he going to have to do to stop her from trespassing on his thoughts? Marry her? Now there's a thought he hadn't thought of before. He hadn't even kissed her yet.

But since last night when he had imagined Henry kissing her, Josiah had given *that* more than one thought. Where could he kiss her, though? It couldn't be in his office. That would be inappropriate. And he couldn't kiss her at the hotel. That wouldn't work out. There had to be an answer, because he felt like he needed to kiss her. Need. He needed to kiss her. The thought amused him. The perfect answer with the perfect solution would turn up. He knew it would.

CHAPTER TWENTY-EIGHT

THE MAN TOOK his Marlboro Lights out of his pocket, opened the glove box, and pulled out the leather pouch of tobacco and rolling papers. He opened the pouch to make sure he already had some rolled and ready. Rolling cigarettes was a chore for him, because he still didn't have the hang of it. Pulling one last Marlboro out of the package, he put the rest of the pack inside the glove box. He closed the door of the truck without locking it. Except for the half pack of cigarettes, there was nothing in it worth stealing.

After double-checking the makeshift corral to make sure it was secure, he mounted his horse and took off down the trail. Ah, how he loved this job. He chuckled at his own joke. Two nights at a hotel for two bucks, decent food, a few beers, and some good poker. All he had to do was act like a good ole boy, chummy up to the sheriff—who didn't suspect anything—and then misappropriate a few cows for one hundred percent profit. He might even make a few more bucks playing poker if he was lucky. And he didn't even have to be too lucky. Those local yokels didn't understand the nuances of the game, so he'd get their money almost every time.

This could go on forever, and he would have no complaints. He could keep this *job* until every cow had disappeared from the county. And all the while helping the sheriff and making sure he stayed away from the trail to the cave. "Oh, Sheriff, I didn't find a thing!" It was like taking candy from a baby. What a great life!

His horse started up the hill, so he knew they were close to the cave. A few minutes later, they entered the cave. The horse, used to the routine, stopped when they came to the fence panel. The man dismounted, secured the panel into place, remounted, and continued to the other side of the cave.

He smiled as they emerged into the sunlight. "Hello, nineteenth century!" he said under his breath. He felt like he had it all: a great gal who treated him like gold, a great job (snicker, snicker), and free money. What could be better?

Several minutes after riding past the Red Bluff sign, he reached town. Riding around the back way, he stopped at the livery stable and dismounted. "Hey, Ezra!" he called.

The young man came out of a stall from the back. "Hallo, Mr. Clinton. Two nights again?"

"Yes, but I'll need him tomorrow morning for a short ride. Can you have him saddled and ready for me by seven?"

"Sure thing, Mr. Clinton. I'll give him a good rubdown right now."

"Thanks, Ezra. Appreciate it." He undid his saddlebags from the saddle, swung them over his shoulder, tossed the young man a quarter, and walked back out into the sunshine. Aw, this is the life, he thought.

Walking briskly down the street toward the main part of town, he thought how lucky he was to have stumbled onto that cave. And he remembered his first visit to town. His first thought was to rob the bank and hightail it back to his own time. He didn't know how much money that would have made him, but this cow deal was so much sweeter. Like a money tree that he could keep returning to again and again.

Opening the door of the hotel, he strode in like he owned the joint. "Hello, Eliza! How is my favorite innkeeper today?" He could charm these poor hicks so easily; he almost felt sorry for them. Not.

"Hallo, Mr. Clinton. How nice to see you again. Two nights or one?"

"Nice to see you again, too, Eliza. Two nights, please." He plunked four half dollars on the counter. "You have any more of those gold pieces to trade?"

"Let's see," she opened the cash register and put his two dollars in. "Yes, it looks like I have three of them." She put them on the counter in front of him. "But I don't know what you see in them. They're worth the same dollar that half dollars are."

"I like looking at them better," he said as he traded his six half dollars for her three gold pieces. He slipped the coins in his pocket, gave her a big smile, and walked upstairs to his room.

After dropping off his saddlebags, he came back downstairs, waved to Eliza, exited the hotel, and walked across the wide street to the saloon. Pushing open the swinging doors, he walked straight to the bar. "Matthew, gimme a beer, please." By this time, he knew almost everyone in town.

Looking around the room, he saw two women that

121

he'd never seen before. Lookers, too, they were. They had a different air about them than most women around here. Had Ole Josiah softened up and let some hookers back in this town? He wouldn't mind a roll in the hay with the one on the right.

Matthew put the beer on the counter. The man handed Matthew a nickel for the beer, and then put a quarter into the tip jar. Last of the big time spenders, he mused! Ha!

He stood at the bar with his beer and watched the women talk and laugh. What was it about them that felt different? Whatever it was, he found them very appealing. It was like they didn't have the naivete of the women around here. They must be hookers. He'd go over and give it a shot. Jingling the coins in his pocket and smiling, he thought, I just might get lucky.

CHAPTER TWENTY-NINE

JENNA AND SARAH had been quietly talking about the Marlboro cigarette when the cowboy walked in. He was good-looking with an arrogance to his walk. They laughed about how attractive all the men in the nineteenth century were.

The cowboy walked toward their table with a grin on his face like he had just won the lottery. Then Josiah came through the swinging doors, smiled at Jenna, and intercepted the cowboy on his way to their table.

"Clinton! Good to see you!" Josiah gave the man a friendly clap on the back. "I haven't seen you since I left for that trial."

"Good to see you, too, Sheriff."

Josiah turned around. "Would you like to meet my two favorite ladies?" He motioned toward Jenna and Sarah. "This is my friend Jenna and her friend Sarah. And Clinton, I apologize, but I keep forgetting your first name."

"It's Hilary."

"Ah, that's right, sorry. Hilary Clinton, this is Jenna, and this is Sarah."

Jenna noticed that Sarah was trying her hardest to suppress a laugh. Jenna hoped that neither "Hilary" nor Josiah would notice that as she smiled and said hello, she was biting the inside of her cheek to keep from laughing.

Hilary Clinton tipped his hat to the two women. Sarah, who sat closest to him, reached up and squeezed his upper arm. She said, "Hilary, it's obvious that you're all man, but isn't Hilary a woman's name?"

"Not in this time—I mean, it depends on the spelling. At least that's what I heard. I spell mine with one el."

Jenna saw Hilary Clinton quickly glance toward Josiah to see if he had caught the slip. He didn't, of course, but she and Sarah had. Wanting to prevent him suspecting anything of the two women, Jenna said, "That makes perfect sense. I think I've heard that, too."

Hilary Clinton tipped his hat toward Jenna and smiled. It looked as if he was ready to sit down with them, when Josiah pulled him a few feet away from the table.

"Hey, Hilary, what do you make of this?" Josiah asked.

Jenna watched as Josiah pulled the Marlboro cigarette out of his shirt pocket and showed it to him. Hilary Clinton made an unconscious movement with his hand and patted his shirt pocket. Jenna could see there was no cigarette pack in it. And she felt certain that was what he was checking for.

"No, Sheriff, I've never seen anything like it. Strange, isn't it? Perfectly round like that," said Hilary.

"Yeah, that's what I thought, too. Plus those words printed on there. Marlboro Lights. What do you suppose that means?"

"I haven't a clue, Sheriff. Do you have any other clues to go with this one?"

124

Josiah hesitated. Jenna thought in his direction as hard as she could—don't mention the cow pies. Don't tell him. Don't tell him. Don't tell him. Josiah must have heard.

"I'm still investigating. I'm sure something will turn up. Say, any chance you can help me search again?"

Hilary's face lit up. "Sure! Not tomorrow, I have some work I have to do, but the next day I'm free."

"Great. Is nine o'clock all right? Do you want to meet at my office like before?"

"Sure."

"Good. We're all set now." Josiah turned toward the table and said, "Jenna, we better get over there. We don't want Eliza to hold supper for us. Sarah, would you like to come to dinner, too? I'm sure there's enough. Eliza always has plenty."

"No, I have to start singing soon. I'll follow you over there, though."

The two women stood up and followed Josiah to the door. He held open one swinging door, and they walked out. Then Josiah put out an arm for Jenna to slide her arm through and put out his other arm for Sarah. "I am walking across the street with the two most beautiful women in town!"

As he walked, he reached over and patted Jenna's arm. When he left his hand there, Jenna put her hand on top of his and smiled at him. He beamed.

When they reached the hotel door, Josiah held it open. Jenna let Sarah enter first. And as Jenna walked through the door, she surreptitiously glanced back at the saloon. Hilary Clinton watched from over the swinging saloon doors.

CHAPTER THIRTY

Sarah walked a few steps toward the staircase and motioned Jenna over to her. "Josiah, I need to talk to Jenna for a few minutes. You know, girl talk."

Josiah nodded and walked into the back room of the hotel. Jenna knew what Sarah wanted to talk about before she even reached her.

"Jenna! I told you before that you had to tell him! Now you know you must! That Hilary Clinton guy is the one coming through the cave and stealing the cattle! You have to tell him!"

"I know that, Sarah. When 'Hilary' said his name, all the pieces fell together. Or, I should say *her* name."

"Where are you going to do it? Not in front of Eliza, I hope. I don't think she's ready for anything like that."

"No, not here. Not at dinner. I have to hope that we can be alone somewhere after dinner. I'll try to arrange it somehow. How I'm going to tell him, I have no idea. How do you tell someone you're from the future? I'd have a hard time believing it now. But someone from the nineteenth century? I'll do my best," Jenna said. She sounded tired.

"Good luck! I have to run now and change clothes."

Jenna smiled at her friend and walked into the back. Although the table was set, Josiah and Eliza stood a few feet away lost in quiet conversation. Samuel came out from the back carrying a tray of food.

"Come on, everyone! Supper is served!"

Josiah parted from Eliza and pulled the chair out so Jenna could sit down. Eliza disappeared into the kitchen, while Samuel sat down. The tray held a red meat dish and some beets. Then Eliza came out of the kitchen with hot rolls. She set them on the table and sat down.

"Oh, Eliza, it looks delicious again! I'm going to have to go on a diet after this."

"Child, you don't need a diet. You are too thin already."

Everyone passed the food around with easy, congenial conversation. Jenna was glad that nothing about where she was from came up. She dreaded having to tell Josiah. But with Hilary Clinton in the picture, she had no choice. After dinner, came delicious cherry pie.

"Eliza, you are outdoing yourself! When do you have time to cook all this?"

"It's not all me. Samuel often helps with cooking, but today it was Dad. He was going to join us for supper, but at the last minute decided that he would rather go hear your friend Sarah sing."

When everyone had emptied their plates and Jenna had said her thank yous, Josiah stood up. "Eliza, Samuel, if you would excuse us, I'd like to take Jenna walking again tonight."

Eliza smiled, and Samuel said, "That a boy!"

Then Eliza said, "Wait a minute, Josiah. I'd like to ask Jenna something. Jenna, will you be coming back next weekend with Sarah?"

"Yes, probably. I hadn't thought about it."

"Well, we'd love to have you over for supper again. We've enjoyed your company so much! How about it?"

Jenna smiled. Eliza made her feel so much at home. "I'd love to, Eliza. But I want to bring the dessert this time. Okay?"

"Deal," said Eliza.

Josiah came around the table and pulled out Jenna's chair to help her up. Then he took her arm and led her out of the hotel.

CHAPTER THIRTY-ONE

DINNER HAD STARTED later so the sun was already going down when they stepped outside. "I've showed you the town, so why don't we go to my office and talk. Is that okay, Jenna?"

"Yes, Josiah, that's fine." His office might be the perfect place to tell him the truth about her—and Hilary.

They walked into his office, and Josiah lit the kerosene lamp that was behind his desk. Then he pulled his chair closer so they were looking right at each other. Jenna wondered what was going on. Now it didn't feel like it was the right time to tell him. Would it ever be the right time? While she wondered, Josiah spoke.

"Jenna, do you know what astronomy is?"

Jenna thought that if she had been drinking a coke, she would have spit it all over him. As it was, a funny squeak escaped from her lips as she tried to contain her laugh. "Um, yes, I do." She couldn't blame him, though. He didn't know that she'd been to college. Few women of the nineteenth century had been.

"Do you like to look at the stars?" he asked, as he looked into her eyes.

"I love looking at the stars and trying to identify the constellations."

"Me, too." He looked out the window. "When it gets dark, if you don't mind staying, I'd like to show you something you might like."

"That sounds good, Josiah." Jenna didn't know what he was thinking, but he had an expectant look on his face. Was he going to ask her to marry him or something? She knew she wasn't ready for that. And would he even want to marry her after he knew the truth about her? She wouldn't know that until after tonight.

"You look like you're somewhere else. What are you thinking about, Jenna?"

"Josiah, I need to tell you something." Jenna thought it might as well be now.

He looked out the window again and stood up. "Can it wait, Jenna? I'd really like to show you the stars."

Jenna welcomed any delay for telling him something she didn't really want to tell him. "Yes, of course, Josiah."

He opened the door to the room he slept in, and then quickly turned back and smiled. "Unless you were about to tell me where you're from?"

Jenna smiled and hung back. "Josiah, not to be an alarmist, but why are we going into your bedroom?"

Josiah's face turned bright red. "Oh! Sorry! Jenna, sorry! The back door is on the other wall. See, you can see it from here." He pointed to the back door. "Or, we can walk around. It's not that far to walk."

"No, Josiah. I see the door. This is fine."

He closed the door after her as she came in and opened the back door for her. It was almost completely dark. She didn't know how he could see anything. Maybe

130

nineteenth-century people had better night vision than she did. What was he going to show her back here? The outhouse?

"It's dark back here, but I can help you. Here, put out your hand. Feel the ladder?"

"Yes, I feel something. What's the ladder for?"

"Jenna, I wouldn't have even thought of this, but you ride horses, and you seem, I don't know, open to possibilities."

"Josiah, what are we doing here in the dark with me holding a ladder?" Jenna demanded. "This is strange!"

"You'll understand in a minute. Now let me go up first, and then you come up. Just follow me up the ladder. I noticed you had boots on, so you shouldn't have any problem. Just be careful."

Jenna moved away, and Josiah stepped quickly up the ladder. She sighed and followed, placing her feet carefully on the rungs and hoping she didn't get a splinter from the handrails. When she reached the top, he helped her up.

"I already put a blanket down."

"Josiah, what are we doing up here?"

"Please, Jenna. Trust me. You'll like this."

"I've heard that before," said Jenna, knowing he wouldn't know what she meant. Well, he was the sheriff of Red Bluff. This Red Bluff anyway. She didn't think he would try to take advantage of her or anything. Although, maybe she could take advantage of him if the situation presented itself! She lay down on the blanket, and he lay on the roof beside her.

"Now, look up there." She thought he pointed upwards, but she couldn't see his hand.

"Ohhh," she gasped. Jenna hadn't seen that many

131

stars since the last time she went camping many years before. Her Red Bluff had too many city lights to see this many stars, even out by where she lived. "It's amazing, Josiah! Thank you for bringing me up here."

"I thought you'd like it. Do you recognize any of them?"

"Although I've always loved looking at the stars, the only ones I know are the Big Dipper, Little Dipper, and Orion. Orion is my favorite."

"I see them. I've always liked Orion, too," said Josiah.

"Do you know the names of any of the others?"

"Hold your arm out." Jenna stretched her arm out, and Josiah guided it. "Over there is Scorpio, do you see it? And there is Cassiopeia, and over there is Draco."

"That's so cool, Josiah. You're amazing."

A second later, Josiah rolled gently on top of her and brushed her lips with his. Surprised and taken off guard, Jenna said, "Oh!"

"I'm sorry, Jenna. Was it bad of me to bring you up in the dark and kiss you like that? You're not angry, are you?"

In response, Jenna rolled onto her side, leaned over, and kissed him gently on the lips. Josiah, taken by surprise, said, "Oh!" And then they both laughed. He took her hand into his, brought it to his mouth, and kissed it.

"I like you," he said.

"I like you, too, Josiah. But I have to ask you something and then tell you something."

"Are you going to acknowledge the corn, now?" He squeezed her hand.

"Acknowledge the corn? What do you mean?"

"You know—admit the truth—tell me where you're from," said Josiah.

"Yes, eventually. You'll think I'm crazy for asking this, but can you tell me what year this is?"

"Yes, Jenna! I think you're crazy! But I still like you! It's 1870."

"Okay, thank you. Next, I want to tell you that I've been to college."

"Really? That's where you learned about astronomy then?"

"It's more than that, Josiah. I'm an attorney."

"You're a lawyer? You're kidding! I didn't know there were any female lawyers."

"There's something else, Josiah. I'm not from around here. Well, actually I am. I was born and raised in Red Bluff."

"But you went away somewhere, and now you're back?"

"No, Josiah. Except for some vacations, I never left. I still live there now."

"You mean here. Wait. What do you mean you live there now? I never saw you before a few weeks ago."

"Josiah, I'm from another time. I'm from the future."

Josiah laughed. "Now you're teasing me. Come on, where are you from?"

"Josiah, I'm not kidding. I'm serious. I came from the future. Those cow pies you found. Were they close to something else that you didn't mention?"

He exhaled sharply, and asked, "What do you mean?"

"The cow pies? My guess is they were on what looked like a wide deer path. And if you took that deer path you would come to something that looked like an opening in the rock. Am I close?"

"So you've been to the cave. What does that prove?" He sounded defensive, and he pulled his hand from hers.

"How far into the cave did you go?"

"Just a few steps. I was already late for supper and thought I'd go back today to check it out, follow it to the end."

"What you would have found was another world, Josiah. My world. A world with cars, trucks, and jet planes."

"What are cars, trucks, and jet planes?"

"A car is like a stagecoach without horses. It goes on its own. A truck is the same only bigger. Jet planes fly through the sky and carry passengers."

"Now I know you're fooling me, Jenna. It's not funny."

Jenna felt for his hand and picked it up in hers. He tried to pull away, and she wouldn't let him. "Josiah, I'm telling you the truth. I know it sounds far-fetched, but it's the truth. I'm telling you the truth. And there's more."

He tried to pull his hand away again, and she wouldn't let him. "Come on, Jenna, let's go back down. This is crazy."

"Hilary Clinton is your cattle rustler."

That got his attention. "How would you know that?"

"That thing that you found? That's a manufactured cigarette. That's how they make them now—I mean where or when I come from. There are all kinds of different brands. Marlboro Lights is one of them."

"Why does that make Hilary the rustler? That makes no sense, Jenna."

"Because Hillary Clinton is the name of a famous woman politician. She was the Secretary of State, a Senator of New York, and before all that she was the wife of President Bill Clinton."

"Two people can have the same name."

"If you had gone farther into the cave, you would

have found a fence panel. It is a large piece of metal meant to hold cattle or horses. One piece of it is against the wall inside the cave."

That got Josiah's attention. "So if this isn't a fairytale you're telling me, then he could set up the fence, put the cattle in the cave with his horse at the entrance to hold them in, and then push any cow pies under the bushes. No one would know he had been there."

"There's more, Josiah. On my side of the cave, there's another trail that leads to the street. A street is—"

"I know what a street is, Jenna."

"A street in my time is a little different. A lot different. It's not made of dirt. Oh, did Boston have cobblestone streets when you lived there?" Josiah nodded. "It's similar to that only flat. Cars and trucks drive on it. When I followed the trail to the street, I found evidence of a makeshift corral—made out of more fence panels like were in the cave—and plenty more cow pies. It's Hilary Clinton, Josiah. I'd bet my life on it."

"So you're from the future, and so is Hilary Clinton?"

"Yes, that's right."

"And Sarah?"

"Yes, Sarah, too. During the week, she works for an attorney. Since I used to be an attorney at that office, I got her the job."

Josiah pulled his hand away. "Let's get out of here. I'll help you down."

"What about what I've told you?"

"Even if it's true, Jenna, how can I catch someone from the future? It's useless."

"No, Josiah, I have a plan. I know it will work."

"Let's get down, and you can tell me as I walk you back to the hotel."

135

Getting down the ladder in the dark was more difficult than getting up. But Josiah was right below her, holding her up and ready to catch her in case she missed a rung on the way down. She felt better when he took her hand to lead her into the building. But when they had stepped in the door, he dropped it. He closed the door behind her and motioned her to sit down by the desk.

"So, what's your plan?" he asked. He sounded tired and disappointed, and he had a touch of anger in his voice.

She explained everything to him in detail. Exactly how it would work and why Hilary Clinton wouldn't get away.

Josiah nodded his head solemnly. "It might work. It might not. But I might as well try as I have nothing else. And although it's a wild, crazy story, maybe you're telling the truth.

"Come on. I need to take you back to the hotel."

Just before they got to the door of the hotel, Jenna turned to him and said, "Aren't you going to kiss me good night?"

"No, Jenna, I'm not. I'll see you in the morning at six in my office. Good-bye." He opened the door for her, let her in, and closed it behind her.

CHAPTER THIRTY-TWO

AFTER SPEAKING BRIEFLY to Eliza about leaving early in the morning, Jenna walked upstairs to the room she shared with Sarah. She lay in bed unable to sleep, the events of the evening playing in her mind. The way Josiah kissed her—and feeling his pleasant weight on top of her for that brief instant. The way she kissed him, wanting more, but resisting. And finally how he had reacted so horribly to what she told him. Jenna had wondered what would happen once he knew the truth about her. Now she knew. She had lost him before he was ever truly hers. Now she just wanted to cry. Sleep was not possible.

Jenna didn't know how long she had lain in bed unable to sleep when she heard voices at the door. It was Sarah's voice and a man's voice. Then a sound of something pushing against the door, and Sarah's voice a little louder with a touch of urgency. Jenna got out of bed and looked around the room. Finally, she picked up one of her cowboy boots, held it behind her, and opened the door.

"Oh, it's you," slurred Hilary Clinton as he pushed

Sarah aside and took a step toward her.

"Get away from me, from both of us, you creep," said Jenna. He was a jerk and a thief, and now he was drunk.

"It's you I wanted all along. Where's your boyfriend, the sheriff? He doesn't know a good thing when he sees it." He made a grab for her.

Jenna brought the heel of the cowboy boot with all her might against his forehead. She hoped it would be enough. There was nothing else in the room to hit him with.

"Ouch! You didn't mean that did you?"

"I meant it, you creep! If you make another move toward either of us, I'm calling Eliza. She'll never let you stay here again."

That got his attention. As he rubbed the sore spot on his forehead where the boot had caught him, he said, "Aw, and I thought you two were a coupla hookers. You're no fun at all. You should go back where you came from." He staggered off down the hall, still mumbling.

Sarah and Jenna walked into their room and pulled the heavy wooden sink in front of the door. "That should keep him out tonight, and tomorrow won't matter," said Jenna.

"What do you mean tomorrow won't matter? You mean because we're leaving?"

"That, too, but Josiah and I have a plan to catch him with the stolen cattle." She explained to Sarah the details of the plan. Then told her that if she happened to see the jerk, Hilary Clinton, in the morning, not to say anything that might tip him off. "Now let's try to calm down and get some sleep. Oh! How am I going to get up at five thirty? I don't have a clock!"

"No problem," said Sarah. She searched through her

bag, pulled out her cell phone, and held it up for Jenna to see.

"You brought your cell phone to the nineteenth century? Come on, Sarah, it won't work here!"

"I can't get calls or texts, but the clock app works fine! Five thirty? Here, I'll set it for you." She tapped something into the face of the smartphone and then handed it to Jenna. "All set."

Jenna shook her head, smiled, and said, "Thank you, Sarah! You're a lifesaver!" Then she lay down in bed and fell right to sleep.

The cell phone rang promptly at five thirty. Jenna shut it off so it wouldn't wake Sarah. She put on her clothes, packed her bag, and left the cell phone in the middle of the bed where Sarah would see it. Then she quietly left the room and gently closed the door.

The kerosene lamps illuminated the staircase and helped Jenna find her way to the door. The sky was slowly beginning to brighten. She had given herself extra time so she could saddle Magic. But when she looked down the street, she saw that he was at the hitching post in front of Josiah's office. Walking down there, she took deep breaths and kept telling herself that if it was meant to be, it would happen. If not, it wouldn't. Now that he knew the whole truth about her, there was nothing she could do about it.

Stopping for a moment to stroke Magic, she thought, "Buck up! You can do this!" And she walked into Josiah's office.

"Good morning, Josiah."

"Morning," he said without looking up.

Great, thought Jenna, he's still in a foul mood. This is going to be a fun day.

"Are you ready to go?"

"Yeah, gimme a minute," he said as he shuffled papers around on his desk. It looked like he moved them from one corner to another without any real purpose. Maybe he was going to dust underneath them or something. Finally, he stood up and looked at her.

"You're still sticking to this crazy story?"

Jenna looked at him with narrowed eyes as she blew a breath rapidly out her nose. Then she turned around and walked out the door, letting it slam behind her. She tied her bag to the back of Magic's saddle and climbed aboard.

Josiah came out the door. "Just checking." He swung up into his saddle and turned his horse toward the cave.

Magic followed the other horse. Both dogs trailed behind. Although the road was wide enough for two horses, Jenna made no move to catch up to Josiah. She didn't need those angry eyes looking at her. The sooner this was finished, the better. She hoped that she was right that Hilary Clinton would bring the cattle through the cave today.

They rode in silence until Josiah and his horse passed the turnoff trail to the cave. "Josiah," Jenna said, "are you testing me? Because you just passed the trail."

He turned his horse around with a sheepish grin on his face. "There could be more than one cave."

Jenna didn't answer and turned her horse to the side trail. She looked behind her with a blank expression when they entered the cave. They came to the fence panel stretched across the path. A feeling of relief swept over her. Yes, Ole Hilary Clinton would be bringing the cattle through today. She was right.

CHAPTER THIRTY-THREE

JOSIAH HAD GOTTEN off his horse and was examining the panel. "This is what they used in your time to contain cattle? It's got no barbs on it."

"Oh, this isn't barbed wire. That's something completely different. Barbed wire is just a thin wire with barbs on it. This paneling is strong enough that it doesn't need barbs."

He lifted the panel and moved it to the side so she could pass. Then he walked his horse through while Jenna waited. After putting the panel back in place across the path, he got back on his horse. They walked the rest of the way out of the cave.

"Are we in your time yet?"

"Yes."

"At what point in the cave does it change over?"

"That's a good question. I have no idea."

They rode down the trail and met the main trail. "Is this the trail to the street that you told me about?"

"No, this is the main trail. There's a chance we might see other riders today, although it hasn't been too busy lately. If it was closer to summer, there would be many people out riding."

Soon, they came to the trail that led to the street. "This is it, Josiah."

He nodded his head, and they rode on. Soon the stock truck came into view. "Wow! It's huge! Is that what you call a car?"

"No, that's a truck. They come in different sizes. There are some much bigger than that. They call them eighteen wheelers, because they have eighteen wheels!"

Josiah slowly shook his head. "I can't imagine such a thing. And there's the corral, just like you said. I shouldn't have doubted you. I'm sorry."

Jenna appreciated his apology, but his tone wasn't any warmer. Back to business. "Josiah, will Bingo bark if someone comes down the trail?"

"No, he shouldn't. Why?"

"I think it's important for us to know when Hilary comes in our direction. We don't want anything to go wrong. So I was going to have Jet wait at the turnoff and come back when she saw him and the cows coming." She still felt silly calling the crook Hilary, but she didn't know what else to call him.

"I'll keep Bingo with me."

Jenna called Jet, and they retraced their steps until they came to the main trail again. "Jet, you stay here until you see someone coming. Don't bark. Just come back and let us know. Okay?" Jet wagged her little nub of a tail and sat down facing the way Jenna had pointed her. She understood.

When Jenna arrived back at the truck and corral, Josiah was off his horse, standing on the truck bumper, and looking into the back. Jenna smiled to see that vehicles intrigued even men of the nineteenth century! Josiah stepped away and examined the corral. "This is really strong. Can we bring some back to my time?" he asked with a smile.

Jenna ignored him and slid off Magic. She tried the passenger door, and it wasn't locked. Pulling herself up into the seat, she sat down and opened the glove box. "Josiah! Score!"

Josiah walked over to her. She held up the box of Marlboro Lights. He put out his hand. "Let me see those things." Looking at the box, he turned it over in his hand and opened and closed the flip top. Then he pulled a cigarette out and examined it carefully. "What is this brown thing on the end?"

"It's called a filter. Nowadays, almost all cigarettes have them."

He sniffed them and handed them back to her. "And look at this, Josiah." She handed him Hilary's cell phone.

"What in the world is this?"

"Another modern invention. Too hard to explain right now."

He handed it back. "We better get ready in case Hilary comes back."

"Josiah, would you give me your rifle?"

"Is this a double-cross or something, Jenna?"

She couldn't help it, she laughed. "Josiah, you need backup here. I know you can handle it in your Red Bluff, but in my Red Bluff, it's a little different. I'm a good shot and not afraid to shoot. Give me your rifle in case something goes wrong."

Grumbling, he walked over to his saddle, pulled the rifle out of its case, and handed it to Jenna.

"Is it loaded?"

"Of course. I'm always prepared."

"A real boy scout, huh?"

"What?"

"Never mind. When Jet comes back, I'll get behind the truck so he doesn't see me. I can hear everything from there and be ready to come out if you need me."

"Okay."

Jenna closed the door of the truck and climbed into the saddle. They walked their horses away from the corral and to the edge of the clearing, so they could see Hilary before he saw them. Then they waited in silence, watching the trail for Jet to return.

CHAPTER THIRTY-FOUR

THE MAN KNOWN as Hilary Clinton smiled to himself. He had a hangover from drinking too much, and it ticked him off that he hadn't gotten lucky with those two girls. But he had money in his pocket and was about to have a whole lot more.

He guided the five cattle up the trail and into the cave. Leaving his horse at the entrance so the cattle couldn't escape, he pulled the whisk broom out of his saddlebags. First he kicked the cow pies under the nearby bushes and put dirt on his boots to remove what had lingered there. Then he used the whisk broom to smooth out the trail, so no one could see the cow tracks.

This had worked so far and would keep working. Everything would be fine as long as that idiot sheriff kept asking him to help find the rustler. It wasn't difficult to get the sheriff to give him this side of town to search. The man wondered how long he could keep up this charade—maybe until all the cattle were gone! Then he would hope the ranchers bought more cattle, and he could do it all again.

Oh, yeah, this was the life. He had heard that someone was selling a ranch close to town. Maybe he should buy it. No one would suspect him then, and he could still be near the cave—and his other life. Maybe he could even get a live-in girlfriend here. Two different worlds, two different women—he'd heard of men doing that, but nobody doing it in two different times! Women in two different centuries! He'd be the first! How cool was that!

He mounted his horse, and they pushed past the cattle until they reached the fence panel. Having done it enough times, the man known as Hilary Clinton leaned over, picked up the fence panel, and leaned it against the side of the cave. Then he backed his horse up so he could keep the cows in front of them—in case they needed incentive. They usually didn't. The dumb animals just wanted to go toward the light.

The five cows, followed by the horse and rider, emerged from the cave and continued down the trail. He smiled again. It wasn't just the free money from the cows anymore. He had charmed and become friends with the woman, Eliza. Now she saved her gold coins for him. A dollar was a dollar to her, but to him it was a fortune. Selling the gold coins to coin dealers in the present had netted him a small fortune. And he didn't have to split that with his buddy, Mac, either. Mac didn't even know about the coins.

Yes, life was good for a sharp man traveling between two centuries. Learn how everything works and make the best out of everything you can. That's what he did. That's why he was good at what he did. He was careful, and he was smart. That idiot sheriff would never catch him. First thing he'd do tomorrow after "helping the sheriff" was check on that ranch for sale. That was a great idea.

The group came to the main trail. The cows must have followed the scent of the many cows that had gone before them, because they walked the correct way down the trail. After tomorrow, he'd take a few weeks off. Let everything cool down.

The five cows turned off onto the side trail like they should. He took a deep breath. Almost a done deal now.

CHAPTER THIRTY-FIVE

JUST WHEN JOSIAH was getting fidgety, he saw the dog coming down the trail. He heard Jenna whisper, "Come on, Jet," and watched her guide the horse behind the truck. Josiah stood his ground. He had already decided he was not going to have his gun drawn when Hilary appeared. That was not the way he did things.

The cows walked down the trail toward him. Jenna may have made him angry with her confession, but she was sharp. She had this all figured out. Then Hilary appeared.

"Ah, Sheriff. What a surprise this is. You know, to see you in my time and all." He reined in his horse as the cows, following tracks and scents of cows before them, walked peacefully into the corral.

"Yes, it is a surprise, isn't it, Clinton? The surprise was on me, though. I was ready to make you my deputy. Imagine that."

Hilary Clinton laughed. "Yes, that would have been perfect." A moment of silence. Hilary looked down and then picked his head back up. "You know, Sheriff, I may be from the future, but I'm still a pretty quick draw. Are

148

you willing to risk it for a few cows?"

"Those cows mean a living for some of our ranchers, Clinton."

"What about you, Sheriff? We're out here away from everybody. How about if I make it worth your while to let me go? I've been making big money off these cows, and I'm a big enough man to share."

"By my count, Clinton, these five cows make your total fifty-four. I figure you owe 'my time' twenty-seven hundred dollars. Pony up!"

"That's crazy! These cows are worth only fifteen or twenty bucks in your time. That's only a thousand dollars. I'll pay you that."

"It's too late to pay what they're actually worth, Clinton. You should have done that in the beginning. If you had paid those ranchers twenty dollars a head, you could have had as many cattle as you wanted. And still made plenty of money. Now you have to make up for the trouble. Mine and theirs." Josiah hoped that Jenna was listening and would realize the situation had gotten shaky. He didn't want to draw his gun, but he was ready to, if needed.

Just then, Jenna rode out from behind the truck, with the rifle drawn and pointed at Hilary. Josiah thought they made a good team. Too bad she was from this weird future.

"'Scuse me, boys. Sorry to interrupt, Josiah, but I thought you might need a little leverage and some insurance."

"You!" said Hilary Clinton. "I might have known it was you, you little bitch!"

"Watch your mouth, Hilary Clinton. I have my finger on the trigger, and I'm a good shot. You owe fifty-three

149

hundred dollars, and you get off scot-free. Pay up, dude," said Jenna.

"And what are you going to do if I don't?"

"Drag your ass back to *my* Red Bluff, and let those ranchers do what they want with you," said Josiah. "Rustlin' people's cows is serious business. Ranchers don't like it when someone takes food off their table." Josiah didn't like what was happening. Although he knew that Jenna had her rifle pointed at Clinton, he felt better knowing his own gun was ready.

"Where am I going to get fifty-three hundred dollars?"

"You better come up with something quick, would be my suggestion." Without taking his eyes off the thief, Josiah rummaged behind him in his saddlebags and pulled out a pair of handcuffs.

"Oh, shit. Okay, okay, I'll get the money. It will take me fifteen minutes."

"Where are you going to get fifty-three hundred dollars in fifteen minutes?" asked Josiah.

Hilary Clinton smiled and reached into his pocket. He pulled out a handful of gold coins and held them up. "Sell four of these little beauties, and I'll have the money to you in a snap. Some are worth hundreds, some thousands, but they average about fifteen hundred dollars."

"Jenna? Is that right?"

"I haven't priced gold coins. That sounds about right. Gold is expensive by the ounce these days."

"How many of those coins do you have there, Clinton?"

"What difference does it make?" said Hilary Clinton, with a touch of anger to his voice.

Josiah slowly lifted his gun and pointed it at the thief. "I said, how many of those coins do you have?"

The man moved the coins from his right hand to his left and reached into his pocket pulling out several more. "Eleven," he said flatly.

"Jenna, go take those gold coins from the man."

"No! I'm not going to give them up! It's not fair. I'll give you the fifty-three hundred, and that's more than enough! I won most of these at poker, and picked up a few more that Eliza traded me."

"And did Eliza know that you could get fifteen hundred dollars each for the ones she gave you?"

"No. What difference does it make?"

"It's called deception, Clinton. And I don't much like deception. Give them to Jenna." Josiah cocked his gun.

As Jenna walked up, Hilary Clinton threw the coins at her. They landed in the dirt. "Now that wasn't nice, Hilary. What would Bill say about that?"

"Who's Bill?" asked Josiah.

"Hillary Clinton's husband."

"You bitch," said Hilary Clinton.

"Count the coins, Jenna. See if there are eleven there," said Josiah.

After picking them up, she counted the coins. "Eleven, as advertised."

"Let's see, four for the ranchers, that leaves seven. Give the man back two coins, Jenna."

"No! Why should I? He's a thief and a jerk!"

"Shut up, bitch, and give me the coins," said Hilary Clinton as he held out his hand.

Jenna looked at Josiah with disbelief. "Why would you do that? He doesn't deserve it! He's already got the five cows that he's going to make pure profit on!"

"Give him the coins, Jenna."

"Josiah, do you know that he came to our room last

151

night and tried—well, you know. I had to hit the bastard over the head with my cowboy boot to get him to leave us alone."

Josiah felt himself tense up. He was angry with Jenna, but he didn't want anyone else messing around with her. Especially like that. He thought maybe she was making it up, but Clinton was rubbing a bruise on the side of his forehead.

"Give him the coins, Jenna. Now. He won't be bothering you or us again. Now, Clinton. Here's the deal. You get the cows. We get the money. We're square. But I'm telling all the ranchers who did this. If you ever show your face in town again, you'll know what to expect. You'll have to find a new gold mine to rob now, you thieving rustler! Now, get out of here." Josiah motioned with his gun toward the corral and the truck. "Jenna, get on your horse and keep your aim on this thief."

Jenna got on her horse with the rifle aimed the whole time. Hilary Clinton walked past them toward the back of his truck. He opened it up, took out the extra fence panels and the ramp, and set them up while Josiah and Jenna watched.

The cows moved easily through the passage created by Hilary Clinton. They walked up the ramp into the truck. Then he took down all the panels and loaded them into the truck. His horse walked up the ramp, and the man closed the door.

He waved to Josiah and Jenna, and said, "Good-bye and good riddance to the nineteenth century!" Getting into the truck and slamming the door, he started the engine and gunned it. The sound made Josiah's horse spook. Magic, used to it, stood still. Then Hilary Clinton drove off in a huff of smoke, squealing his tires all the way down the street.

Neither of the two people on horses said a word for a few minutes. Then Josiah said, "Jenna, cash that money and bring it when you come next weekend. We'll give the ranchers the hundred dollars each for the cows they lost, and you can have most of the rest."

"Okay," said Jenna. "Here's your rifle." She handed him the rifle and then continued, "Josiah, would you like to come see my ranch? It's down the way not too far."

He looked at her sternly, still feeling angry. "No, Jenna. I'm going back home now. To *my* time. Where I belong. Good-bye." His horse walked forward, and the dog, Bingo, followed. Josiah didn't turn around.

CHAPTER THIRTY-SIX

JOSIAH ARGUED WITH himself on the ride home. Why did he treat Jenna so rudely? Because he was angry. But was he angry with her for telling him the truth, or angry with himself for not wanting to hear it? He decided it was the latter.

But there was also a part of him that thought if he was mean enough to her that she would go back to her own time and stay there. That way he wouldn't have to see her. If he didn't see her, then maybe this blasted longing for her would go away. He hoped so, anyway.

Could the longing go away after what had happened on the roof? When she kissed him back, it was more than he could take. He loved the feeling of her soft lips on his. It was so unexpected and so welcome.

Dang the woman! He didn't know exactly what it was about her that made him feel like this. It wasn't a feeling he liked. Josiah Stone was always in control. That was something he could depend on about himself. He liked that about himself. And here comes this woman, from the future no less, and takes all his control away.

He supposed he should apologize for treating her like

that. She had only told him the truth. He couldn't blame her for doing that. But if he apologized, he wouldn't want her to think everything could go back to the way it was before he knew. Their friendship, or whatever it was between them, could never go back to the way it was.

He lived here, in the past, and she lived in the future. There was no hope for two people living in two separate worlds. She even owned a ranch there. Her life was there. His home, this time, was only weekend entertainment for her. Jenna wouldn't live here, and there was no way he could live in her world.

Besides, she didn't understand him anyway. She didn't understand why he gave the thief those two gold pieces. His father had always emphasized kindness above all else. But it wasn't just that. His father had also told him that you don't leave a man with nothing.

It was good advice. If he had left Hilary Clinton, or whatever his name was, with nothing, there was a good chance he'd come back to Red Bluff, maybe with some friends, to cause trouble. Josiah couldn't allow that to happen. This way, he may not have been happy when he left. But the five cows and the two coins would at least satisfy Hilary Clinton.

Josiah's main focus right now had to be to get the woman out of his mind. And his heart. He knew he could do it; although he wasn't sure he wanted to. But he had to. There was no future for two people separated by more than a hundred years.

He forced himself to think of something else. Should he get the ranchers together or ride out to see each one individually? It would be easier riding out to see them. It would take him a while, but it would get his mind off what he didn't want to think about anyway.

He'd tell the ranchers who the rustler was. Then, when Jenna got back to town, he'd give them the money for the stolen cattle. He'd have to give Jenna credit for breaking the case. Although he wouldn't tell them about the cave or the time difference, he'd say that Jenna recognized the cigarette, and that was the clue that he needed. He'd also tell them that part of the deal was that Hilary Clinton never show his face in Red Bluff again. So if they saw him, they needed to let Josiah know immediately.

The money—more than six times what the cattle were worth—would satisfy the ranchers. But he wouldn't tell them how much money until he gave it to them. That would be better.

There. It wasn't so hard. He had gone nearly five minutes without thinking about kissing her. Without remembering how kissing her had made his whole body feel. He shook his head trying to dismiss the thoughts.

Then he remembered the scene by the truck, when he and Jenna both had their guns pointed at the thief. What had Jenna said? That he had tried to get into their room last night. The thought made Josiah tense up and have second thoughts about letting the guy go. Although he didn't want Jenna, he didn't want that thief to have her, either. Jenna hit him with her boot. Josiah laughed. That's my Jenna. She's tough.

Josiah thought that his mother would like Jenna. She'd like her spirit, her originality, and her strength. His mother would like everything about Jenna. Just like he did.

He especially liked her kiss. She'd be a lot easier to forget if he hadn't kissed her. And knowing that she kissed him back made it that much more difficult.

They were almost all the way home. Patches had just passed the Red Bluff sign. Josiah sighed a deep, hopeless sigh. Maybe forgetting about her wasn't going to be as easy as he hoped it would be.

CHAPTER THIRTY-SEVEN

Jenna felt despondent on the ride home. She had broken this big case for Josiah, and still he treated her like dirt. He treated Hilary damn Clinton better than he had treated her. And the way he had ordered her to cash the money and bring it back to him. Maybe she just wouldn't go back to his Red Bluff at all. Maybe she'd keep the money. Then what would he tell the ranchers about the money? That would serve him right.

She knew she couldn't do that. Not only was she not a thief, but she needed to go back. Even in the two weekends she'd spent there, it had begun to feel like home. Although she didn't want to admit it, she knew exactly why. Eliza's kindness. The way the older woman treated her felt like mothering to her. Jenna hadn't felt anything like that since losing her own mother. If she never went back there, she would miss Eliza.

And the kiss. Why oh why did he kiss her? That whole episode on the roof made it difficult to forget her feelings about him. It would have been much easier to move on if that kiss had never happened.

Jenna passed through the gate, locked it, and continued to the barn. She unsaddled Magic and put him in his stall. Since he had been cooped up in a stall all weekend, she expected him to go out to the pasture. But Magic just wanted to eat. Jenna hugged his neck and walked into the house.

There were two voicemail messages from her brother, Ryan. Probably more girl troubles. Not needing to hear that right now, she tapped her grandmother's number into the phone.

"If you're looking for money or want me to buy anything, hang up and don't call again. If you want me to drive you somewhere, but you're not willing to give me gas money, go find another sucker. If you think I'm late on one of my bills, you have the wrong number. If you want to tell me how wonderful I am, please leave a message." Beep!

Jenna laughed. Granny and her messages. She was a character. And she was the one who had made life bearable after Jenna's parents had died. Granny had just lost a daughter, but she acted like Jenna was the only one in the world grieving. There was no one like Granny.

"Granny! You're wonderful! Call me when—"

"Hello, Jenna! How are you, darling girl?"

"Granny! You're monitoring your calls now?"

"Oh, Ruth wanted me to play bridge, and she kept nagging and nagging. I finally got her off the phone, but I wasn't taking any chances. But forget about her. What about you? What have you been up to?"

"Granny, you wouldn't believe it!"

"I'm gullible," she giggled. "Try me."

"Well, I'm in love again." The words surprised Jenna. She had never said them aloud or even thought them, but there they were.

159

"I hope he's not a jerk like Daniel! I never liked him. You know that, don't you? I warned you about him."

"No, Granny, he's not a jerk. And I know you never liked Daniel *and* that you warned me about him. You were right, of course."

"You remember that, girl. Now tell me about this new man of yours."

"It's a long story," warned Jenna.

"I'm not dying yet!"

Jenna laughed. She could always count on Granny to give her a few laughs. Starting from the freak snowstorm and the cave, she told Granny the whole story, including the kiss on the rooftop, Josiah's bad reaction to where she was from, and catching Hilary Clinton.

"He's in love with you, too, Jenna. I can tell that from what you've told me. And I like that he gave two coins back to President Clinton's wife."

"I don't understand why he did that. Why do you like that?"

"If he had taken everything from the jerk, then the jerk would have been ticked off and probably gone back to the past to cause trouble. He sounds like he was a troublemaker. That kind want to get revenge. But after Josiah was square with him, he won't be back. Your Josiah did the exact right thing. Bright boy. I like him."

"You haven't even met him!"

"I don't need to. I like him. And I can see why you do, too."

"So what should I do, Granny? He's treating me like he never wants to see me again."

"He doesn't want to see you again! Because seeing you reminds him of what he feels for you. Don't be surprised if he asks you to go back to your own time and never return to his. Don't be surprised—and then ignore him. Wear the most beautiful dress you can find. Get his heart beating. He'll be begging you to stay before you know it."

"Do you think so, Granny? Because right now it feels hopeless."

"No, darling Jenna. Not hopeless. Trust that it will happen and it will."

"Really? Because I wasn't going to go back."

"What about the money?"

"I could give it to Sarah to return to him."

"Jenna, if you're in love with this Josiah dude, then you need to go back. Listen to your ole Granny. He'll be beggin' you to come back. You have to be patient."

Jenna stayed silent.

"So when do I get to meet said cowboy," asked Granny.

"Well, he doesn't want to come here. So, I don't know how you could."

"Why can't I go there?"

"Because the only way to get there is by horse."

"And you think I can't ride?" Granny said indignantly.

"You haven't ridden in years."

"Girl, I was riding horses before you were a sparkle in your grandfather's eye. I could rope a cow when I was five. By seven I had won fourteen barrel races. Should I go on?"

"And now you're seventy-four, and you haven't been on a horse in years."

"You don't forget how to ride a horse, Jenna. It's not like that. I'll bet I can still outride you."

Jenna didn't take the bait. "Okay, Granny, I'll figure something out." She paused. "Granny, I have a question. When I told you that I had gone into the past, it didn't surprise you at all. Why not?"

"You know why, Jenna."

"Because you've been there."

"Once. And something horrible happened. I never went back and never told anyone about it."

"Oh."

"Enough about me. When are you going back?"

"Eliza invited me for supper for Friday. I'm bringing dessert!"

"That should be interesting! Okay, Jenna. Keep me current on the cowboy saga."

"I will, Granny. Love you. Bye.

"Love you, too, girl. Bye."

CHAPTER THIRTY-EIGHT

JOSIAH WAS IN a bind, and he knew it. After passing the Red Bluff sign, he had turned Patches around so he could visit the two ranchers on this side of town. It was still early, and it would save him a ride out there later in the week.

The first rancher, on whose ranch Josiah had discovered the cigarette, was overjoyed that Josiah had found the culprit, *and* that he'd be paid for his losses. But when Josiah told him that Jenna was the one who solved the case, the rancher insisted that Josiah *and* Jenna come over for a celebration supper.

With the second rancher, it was almost the identical story. Celebration supper with Josiah and Jenna. How could he get away from her if he had to keep eating supper with her? How could he not think about her if he had to see her all the time?

There was only one solution. He'd have to ask her, as a personal favor, not to return to *his* Red Bluff. He hated to have to go that far, but he felt like he had no choice. It was drastic, and it would make Jenna feel even worse, but he couldn't stand to look at her anymore. She did things to him. Made him feel things he didn't want to feel. It was his only choice.

With that settled, he could now move on. Maybe he hadn't given the women in town a chance. The best way to forget one woman was to get yourself another woman. At least that's what he'd heard.

After getting Patches settled at the livery, he walked toward the schoolhouse. The last of the children were leaving. Perfect timing, Josiah. Getting over Jenna will be easy!

He walked into the schoolroom. "Hallo, Annie!"

She was erasing the chalkboard and jumped at the sound of his voice. "Hallo, Sheriff," she said, as she continued erasing the board.

"Have you found a buyer for your ranch, yet?"

"I've had one person look at it who wants to look again next weekend."

"Somebody from around here?"

"I promised I wouldn't say."

Josiah found that curious, but he let it go. "Well, be sure to let me know so I can help Rawlins move."

"Yes, Sheriff, I will." She had finished the board, so she sat down at her desk and picked up a book to read.

"Ah, Annie?"

Lifting her head slightly, and without a trace of a smile on her face, she said, "Yes, Sheriff?"

"Would you like to go to supper some time?"

She blinked her eyes as if to get the cobwebs out and said, "Why?"

Flabbergasted, Josiah said, "Nice talking to you, Annie. Good-bye." He walked out the door shaking his head. Doomed. He was doomed to loving a woman he couldn't have. No! There was one more chance.

With his head held high with optimism, he walked into the hotel. When he saw Eliza at the front desk, he said, "Eliza, where is Mary Elizabeth on this fine day?"

"Josiah, what happened with Jenna? She left early this morning and didn't tell me why. I'm concerned for her."

"She's fine, Eliza. Now where's Mary Elizabeth?"

"Josiah Stone! I need more of an explanation than that. And I also want to know why, when you've had your eye on Jenna, why you are suddenly after Mary Elizabeth?"

Feeling frustrated, Josiah almost got short with her, but didn't. "Jenna and I caught the cattle rustler this morning."

Eliza clapped her hands! "That's great! Why was Jenna involved? Oh, no! She didn't get hurt, did she?"

"No, Eliza, Jenna is fine. She identified the cigarette and knew something else as well."

"Are you going to tell me what it was?"

"It's hard to explain, Eliza. Can you tell me where I can find Mary Elizabeth?"

"You haven't told me what's going on with you and Jenna yet," said Eliza, as she arched her eyebrows.

"It wouldn't work between us, Eliza. That's all. It wouldn't work any more than you could catch a weasel asleep. I can't tell you any more. Now I want to find Mary Elizabeth. Will you help me or not?"

Eliza shook her head and frowned. "I don't like this, Josiah. Jenna is a good girl. Samuel and I really like her."

"I like her, too, okay? But it's not going to work. Mary Elizabeth?"

"She went to the store and should be returning shortly."

"Thanks, Eliza. Bye."

165

Josiah walked out the door and crossed the street. He had never seen Mary Elizabeth in the saloon, but glanced in to be sure. As he turned around, he saw her coming down the street towards him.

He smiled broadly at the woman. "Hallo, Mary Elizabeth! How are you today?"

"I'm fine, Sheriff. And you?"

"I'd be great if you'd agree to have supper with me tonight. That is, if you're available."

"Sheriff, I am available—"

"Great! Six o'clock all right?"

"Like I was saying, Sheriff, I am available, but I am not interested in having supper with you."

Josiah's smile faded. "Why not?"

"Because you are the sheriff."

"So? I'm allowed to have supper out."

"That's not my concern, Sheriff. Most sheriff's have short lifespans, and I'm not interested in becoming a widow."

"Mary Elizabeth, it's only supper."

"My answer is no, Sheriff. Good day."

She nodded her head, walked past him, and crossed the street to the hotel. His eyes followed her as he slowly shook his head from side to side. I'm doomed. The only woman who wants me, and who I want, is not available. What am I going to do? What am I going to do? He kept repeating that all the way back to his office and continued after he sat down and put his head in his hands.

CHAPTER THIRTY-NINE

AFTER SPEAKING WITH Granny, Jenna felt much better. Granny always made her feel better. That's what Grannies were for! She tapped out Ryan's number on her phone.

"Hello!"

"Ryan, it's me."

"Hey, Jenna, thanks for calling."

"What's up, Ryan?"

"Wanted you to be the second to know. I dumped Tiffany."

"Oh, hallelujah! What'd she do this time?"

"You wouldn't believe it!"

"Yes, I'm sure I would, Ryan."

"She leaned a chair against this beautiful painting that I had just finished. The painting was still wet, and now it has a big bar across the top where the chair leaned against it."

"Ryan, why does this surprise you? Should I count the ways? She never showed any interest in your artwork. She never took you seriously. She never took anything seriously except her clothes!"

"Don't be so hard on her. Tiffany is a nice girl."

"You just dumped her!"

"Yeah, well."

"Is that what you had to tell me?"

"Yes, and if you know anyone to fix me up with, let me know."

Jenna laughed. "You don't let grass grow under your feet, do you?"

"I'm a man, Jenna. What can I say?"

"Ryan, do you have a few minutes? I have a long story to tell and a favor to ask."

"Sure. I'm good. Go for it."

Ryan may have been bad with women, but he was a good listener. Jenna told him the entire story, and he didn't say one word until she finished.

"Jenna! I've been in that cave!"

"But you never made it to Red Bluff?"

"No. When I got to the other side, it looked like a normal place, so I turned around and went home. Guess I shoulda spent more time there!"

"Ryan, would you mind going over there and checking out the ranch for me? See if it's well-built and all? See if you can make some changes for me?"

"Sure, Jenna, I can do that. It sounds like an adventure. Hey, would you mind if I bring Nick? He'd enjoy a place like that."

"That's fine, Ryan. I appreciate you helping me out like this. I'll invite Kat, too, if you don't mind her tagging along. I asked her before but she had to work."

"No, that's fine. I gotta go now. We'll connect later in the week and arrange everything. Bye, Jenna!"

"Bye, Ryan. Thanks!"

Nick was Ryan's best friend since childhood. They

used to do carpentry together before her brother bought the art store. Now Nick was a cop in Red Bluff. Jenna's sister, Kat, had always had a crush on him. Kat had never told her that, but Jenna always knew. If Kat knew that Nick was going, she might be persuaded to come, too. And Jenna knew that Kat would enjoy all the history over there. Kat loved history.

She tapped out Kat's number. Busy signal. She'd try again later. Jenna knew what she had to do now.

After turning on her computer, she walked to the kitchen to get some water and an apple. She hadn't had breakfast today, and she was hungry. But she didn't have time to fix anything now. She had to look up something.

Jenna opened her browser, and Google popped up. Since she was already familiar with several genealogy sites, she knew exactly where to go. She keyed in Josiah's name, and hesitated. Wait. She'd been here often enough to know the format of the results. The name and dates were at the top, and right underneath, the wife and children were listed. No, it wasn't right to know that. If she wasn't the wife, she didn't want to know. And if she was the wife, she didn't want to mess up the timeline by already knowing that. Finding out about his death was one thing. Finding out about his wife was in another category. She grabbed a paperback book and held it up to the screen. That would shield from her view what she didn't want to know. A few clicks and keystrokes later, and a feeling of relief swept over her. Josiah Stone died in 1910 when he was seventy-five years old. Seventy-five may not be old now, Jenna thought, but in 1910, it was considered old. So, he didn't die in a gunfight. One less thing to worry about. Now all Jenna had to do was stay patient and hope that Granny was right about Josiah's feelings. Time would tell.

While she was looking, she decided to poke around a little more. She looked up William McKenna, and found that yes, he had died in Virginia, in July of 1861. Then she looked up Brian McKenna, Eliza's older son. Surprise! He didn't die until 1906! And he died in Red Bluff! Jenna didn't know what to do. She had no idea how to tell Eliza this news. It was good news, but unsettling. Eliza was right. Her son was still alive. Jenna decided she would keep it to herself for now.

CHAPTER FORTY

ANOTHER DAY AND Josiah had more thoughts of Jenna. Josiah hated this. She wouldn't leave his mind no matter what he did. He'd have to try harder. A union between them was not possible, and he'd have to live with that. If he could. Memories of her kiss still haunted him.

He mounted Patches and set off to visit two of the ranchers on the other side of town. Why did he have to kiss her? If he hadn't done that, and especially if she hadn't kissed him back, forgetting her would be that much easier. As it was, every other thought was about her. And if he had to see her again, it would make it even worse.

That confirmed in his mind that he must ask her not to return here. It shouldn't affect her much—she had never even been here before a few weeks ago. By now she'd probably come to the same conclusion that he had: there was no future for the two of them together.

He tied Patches to the hitching post in front of the rancher's house. The man's wife told Josiah the rancher was in the barn. Thirty minutes later, and after much back slapping and grinning, Josiah left. Unfortunately, this rancher had the same request—no, *demand*—as the other two ranchers. Josiah *and* Jenna *must* come for supper.

It made Josiah want to scream! What was going on? It was like the universe was conspiring against him. Josiah rode to the next ranch. Angry. They had no business butting in to his personal life like this. He wouldn't stand for it. He'd tell them that she had to return to wherever it was she came from, and sorry, but they'd never see her again. Just take your money and shut up.

Josiah visited two more ranches that day, and both of them insisted on the same supper arrangement. The ranchers felt grateful about him finding the culprit and stopping the rustling, and especially about getting paid for the lost cattle. And they didn't even know yet how much they were getting. Maybe if he told them that part of the story, they'd forget about asking him and Jenna to supper.

Hell! In a fit of anger he threw his hat to the ground. Patches sidestepped it and kept walking. Bingo sniffed it and walked on. Josiah had to rein in the horse so he could dismount and retrieve the danged hat. This was ridiculous—getting this worked up over a woman. Never in his life had this happened before. Why now? Why with her? She was just one more woman. From the future. Beautiful. With soft lips and a warm smile. Stop it! Stop it! Stop it!

"What'd ya say, Sheriff?" asked someone from the street. Josiah had entered the edge of town and had no idea he had spoken aloud.

"Nothing, sorry, nothing," he replied, and let Patches walk toward the livery. When they arrived, Ezra wasn't around, so he unsaddled Patches and gave him a quick rubdown. Since the corral was empty, he turned the horse out there, so he could have some room to run.

Then, dejected, with his head down, Josiah walked toward the main part of town. Shuffling along, his lips in a pout and groaning to himself, he made his way to the saloon. He pushed open the doors, saw Matthew behind the bar smiling, and decided against going in. Walking across the street, he opened the door to the hotel and walked in.

"Hallo, Josiah," said Eliza. "What are you looking so grumpy about?"

"Jenna. I'm going to ask her not to return here."

"You can't do that," said Eliza.

"Why not?"

"Because I like her, and I enjoy her company. She's my friend, too, Josiah, and I forbid you to ask her that." Josiah's eyebrows raised in a look of astonishment. "Well, that was a little harsh. Sorry. But you got my ire up, Josiah! How dare you ask her to leave just because you're feeling a little melancholy!"

"I am not feeling melancholy, Eliza! It's just that I want her out of my life, because there is no way she can be in my life."

"And why not?"

"It's something I can't get into. You'll have to ask Jenna."

"Josiah, every romance has its obstacles. That makes it that much sweeter when you get it all worked out. Don't give up now. You two are perfect for each other."

"Not so perfect as you think, Eliza."

"So what happened with Mary Elizabeth?"

"She turned me down."

"Why?"

"Because I'm a sheriff, and she doesn't want to be a widow! Isn't that crazy? I just asked her to supper."

"You know, I mentioned that danger to Jenna, and it didn't bother her at all."

"It can't happen with Jenna."

"And what happened when you talked to Annie?"

"How do you know that I talked to Annie?"

"Because I figured if you were trying to force yourself to get interested in other women, that you would talk to Annie, too. What happened with her?"

Josiah smiled a sad smile. "When I asked her to have supper with me, she said, 'Why?' So much for that!"

"Josiah, dear, I think you ought to give this some thought before you decide that it won't work between you and Jenna."

"I can't stop thinking about her, Eliza. I've been trying to stop, and the thoughts just keep coming."

"You know why, don't you, dear?" Josiah just looked at her, so she continued. "You're in love with Jenna, Josiah. Can't you see that?"

"I am not! I just barely met her. And I came over here to tell you that I won't be at supper Friday night. Sorry." He walked toward the hotel door.

"Josiah, I'm not accepting that. Samuel will feel disappointed, too. I would consider it a personal favor if you came to supper as usual Friday night."

"Oh, Eliza."

"Don't 'oh Eliza' me, Josiah Stone. You need to be there. Tell me you will be."

"Oh, Eliza, okay! But I won't talk! And I won't look at her! Good-bye!"

Josiah walked out and stomped down the street toward his office. He wouldn't look at her because looking at her made him feel worse. It made him want her even more. He couldn't look at her and get over her. It was impossible. Eliza didn't understand. Maybe she would if she knew the obstacle was that the two people lived in two different centuries.

You can't ask a man to do what a man cannot do. He'd show up for supper, but he'd do his best not to let Jenna Leyton affect him. Josiah had a bad feeling that his best wasn't good enough.

CHAPTER FORTY-ONE

AFTER GETTING OFF the genealogy site, Jenna clicked her way directly to eBay. She found two beautiful "old time" dresses, and both of them available with expedited shipping. They needed to arrive by Friday if she was to follow Granny's advice to wear a beautiful dress. If that's what it took to get back on Josiah's good side, then that's what she would do.

She wanted him. And if Granny was right, he wanted her, too. How could she convince him they were right for each other? One thing she knew for sure. She would not tell him that she was considering buying Annie's ranch. Jenna felt that telling him wouldn't be fair. It was honest, but not fair. Josiah had to decide on his own that they could be together. The ranch should not be a factor. Jenna had asked Annie to keep it a secret, and as quiet as the girl was, she didn't think it would be a problem.

She didn't want to wait until Friday to see him again, but it also made her nervous. Granny had also said that he might tell her never to come back. What would she do if he did that? Did she have the strength to ignore him even though it would hurt her very deeply? Jenna took a deep breath. Yes! She did have the strength! She was woman; she was invincible!

When Thursday came around, Jenna felt prepared. Or as prepared as she could be for the unknown. Although the only unknown was Josiah's reaction to her. Otherwise, she knew that Eliza would welcome her and make her feel at home.

She had gone to the two coin dealers in Red Bluff and one in a neighboring town, and still didn't have enough 1800s silver coins to cover the nine gold coins. One dealer in Red Bluff had told her he would order more quarters and half dollars for her. So, she could get them eventually, but not yet.

Ryan, Nick, and Kat would all be riding over Saturday to look at Annie's ranch. They were all excited about seeing the prospect of a "real" 1800s town. Nick, ever the cop, wanted to bring his gun "just in case," but luckily, Ryan talked him out of it.

Next, Jenna stopped at the best bakery in town to see what kind of super dessert she could bring back to impress everyone. The two layer cake with alternate squares of chocolate and vanilla was perfect. She didn't think they baked anything like that way back then. Everyone would like that. And she bought a hard plastic cake tote to keep it safe on the trail. The plastic wouldn't fit into their time, but Jenna figured they'd be too busy eating cake to notice.

Last, she bought a half gallon of Rocky Road ice cream. Did they even have ice cream back then? Maybe, but probably not with those little miniature marshmallows and nuts in it. That should be a hit, too. That would go in the soft sided cooler that she bought. A bunch of ice should keep it frozen and maybe even still solid the following day.

Late Friday afternoon when Sarah arrived, everything was ready to go. Jenna had even brushed and saddled Sarah's horse so they could leave right away.

"Oh, you are rarin' to go, aren't you?" asked Sarah.

"I want to find out if there's anything between Josiah and me, or if it was all a fantasy."

"I can't believe you're thinking of buying that ranch! Once you tell him that, he should be fine."

"I'm not telling him that. It wouldn't be fair. He has to decide on his own. Please don't tell him or anyone else about the ranch, Sarah. The only ones who know are Annie and Eliza. They both said they wouldn't tell."

"You could really live there—full-time?"

"It's what I've always wanted. You know, to live back in the cowboy times. I thought you wanted that, too," said Jenna.

"Well, and it's a big well, I did say I wanted it. But it's one thing to say you want it when it's not possible, and another thing to want it when you've had to go to the bathroom in those smelly, drafty outhouses!"

"Yes, the outhouses. I wasn't thrilled with that at Annie's ranch, either. But, Ryan and Nick are coming to look at it on Saturday. Maybe they'll come up with an idea so I don't have to freeze my butt off in the winter every time I go to the bathroom."

"Good luck with that one!"

Then Sarah told Jenna all about how she was getting over being in love with her boss and how she had considered signing up for online dating. Their conversation rambled on about men and men and men. Soon, they passed the Red Bluff sign.

Sarah wanted to go directly to the saloon, so Jenna

took the horses the back way to the livery stable. Halfway there, she remembered the cooler and her bag full of new dresses; she couldn't carry them that far. To avoid walking in front of Josiah's office, she continued past the livery and rode up the far side of the block. Then she stopped the horses in front of the hotel.

Carrying the cooler, she opened the door of the hotel and held her breath. There was always the chance that Josiah would be inside. She felt thankful that he wasn't. Eliza took the cooler, looked at it strangely, and asked Jenna if she needed more help.

Jenna said no, then walked back outside to get her other bag and Sarah's bag. After leaving them with Eliza, she said she'd be right back.

Ezra, having seen her walk by before, met her at the front of the livery. He took the horses and promised to rub them down.

As fast as she could, Jenna got back into the hotel where she hoped she'd be safe. Eliza gave her the room key, and Jenna carried the two bags upstairs. Eliza had already taken the cooler into her kitchen.

When Jenna returned downstairs, Eliza said, "What is that thing that you brought? I've never seen anything like it. It's cold!"

Jenna smiled. "Eliza, you're going to have to trust me on this one. Don't even ask! It's too difficult to explain."

"That reminds me of something else, Jenna. It's none of my business, except I know you like the man. So why does Josiah think there is an impossible obstacle between you?"

Jenna smiled weakly at Eliza and shrugged her shoulders. "I can't tell you yet, Eliza. Maybe someday."

"Okay, but tell me this. Do *you* think it's an impossible

179

obstacle?"

"No, Eliza, I don't. I'm sorry that he does."

"Josiah came to me to say he was going to ask you not to come back."

Jenna's stomach lurched. Granny was right.

"What?" asked Eliza.

"Oh, I didn't realize I had said anything. I was thinking that my grandmother was right. I talked to her about it when I—when I got back to town last week—and she said that he might do that."

"And what did your grandmother suggest you do about it?"

"Ignore it! But I'm not sure I can do that."

"Your grandmother is a wise woman, Jenna. Josiah *is* in love with you, and I think you're in love with him. You're going to have to be patient while he discovers that he can't do without you."

"That's pretty much what Granny said. She said I should wear a beautiful dress so he would have to look at me! So, I brought two new ones today!"

"I'd like to meet your grandmother one day, Jenna. I completely agree with her. And I'll add this. Sometimes, men need a little prodding. I'd suggest trying to make him jealous."

"Tomorrow, my brother and his friend are riding over to look—" Jenna glanced around the room and lowered her voice, "to look at Annie's ranch for me. Josiah doesn't need to know he's my brother, right?"

"Smart girl. You'll get him back yet. Don't lose hope. I'll do whatever I can to help! Josiah doesn't have to know I'm in cahoots with you!" Eliza and Jenna laughed.

CHAPTER FORTY-TWO

JOSIAH FELT MISERABLE. The moment he had been dreading was almost here. He'd have to leave for the hotel in a few minutes. And then he'd have to see *her*. How could he forget her and move on if he had to keep seeing her? He would have to talk to Eliza again about asking Jenna not to return to Red Bluff. *His* Red Bluff. Let her stay in her own Red Bluff.

What right did she have to come into his time and disrupt his life like this? Come into his time and *kiss* him? How dare she! And yet, he longed to feel those soft lips on his once again. What he would give not to know where she was from. Then he could imagine he and Jenna happily together instead of separated by more than a century.

Supper was at six o'clock. Josiah had waited until six before he ever left his office. That way, he'd be sure that Jenna was already at the table, so he wouldn't have to see her walk across the room. Seeing her from the waist up wasn't half as bad as seeing her walking toward him. Her beauty was almost tangible. No, he'd come late and wouldn't have to see the allure of her beauty.

He left his office and dawdled down the street toward the hotel. Josiah thought that if he walked any slower, he'd fall over. Although he had told Eliza that he'd come to supper tonight, he didn't have to like it. And he was going to make good on his threat not to talk and not to look at Jenna. Eliza could make him come to supper, but she couldn't make him talk or look. How could he keep from looking at beautiful Jenna sitting across the table from him? He'd find a way. He had to.

Josiah walked into the sitting room where the table was, and his heart sank. Samuel was there, but Eliza and Jenna were in the other room. He'd sit down and wouldn't look up when she walked into the room. He could beat this yet.

"What's with you, Josiah? You look like you lost your best friend," said Samuel. Josiah grumbled something, and Samuel said, "What?" Then the kitchen door opened. "Oh, here come the girls."

Josiah's head snapped up as if it had a mind of its own. He gasped. She wore a new dress with a low neckline, and she had never looked more beautiful. He stood up to be polite. Jenna walked over to the table, set down the platter of food, and smiled sweetly at him. Then she sat down, deliberately smiling at him the entire time.

She was killing him. He'd be dead before the end of supper. He knew better than to come to dinner tonight. And now it would take all the self-control that he had not to look at her.

"Josiah? Did you want some chicken?" asked Eliza.

"Hmmm? Oh, yeah. Thank you." He took two pieces of chicken and put them on his plate. After using his fork to cut a piece off, he put it in his mouth, and that's the last he remembered about supper. He couldn't take his eyes off her. And his thoughts were running wild. Stop! Stop! Stop!

"Stop what, Josiah?" asked Samuel.

"Oh, did I say that aloud? Sorry. I just didn't want to eat anymore," lied Josiah. He wasn't a liar, but he didn't have much of a choice there. The truth wasn't something he could talk about. Luckily, the interruption had broken her spell on him. Feeling more normal and in control again, he pushed his plate away and said, "Sorry, everybody, but I need to leave early tonight. Thanks for dinner, Eliza." He stood up.

"Josiah, you have to stay for dessert. Jenna brought it specially from—wherever it is that she's from!" Samuel laughed. Josiah felt helpless. "Jenna, come into the kitchen with me, dear." Eliza picked up the empty platter and a couple of plates and walked into the kitchen. Jenna grabbed the rest of the plates and followed Eliza.

Oh, no, thought Josiah. He'd have to watch her walk in again. Once more her beauty would intoxicate him. He had to leave. Now. He pushed away from the table and stood up, but it was too late. Jenna walked in. Josiah couldn't force himself to look away. He wanted to drink in every fiber of her being. Of her beauty. Trying to breathe, the breath caught in his throat.

"I've brought ice cream and cake," said Jenna.

"You made this yourself, Jenna?" asked Samuel.

"No, store-bought. I just brought it with me."

"Josiah, cake and ice cream?" asked Eliza. He stood there, helpless. "Josiah, you can sit down and close your mouth now."

Josiah sat down and noticed that Eliza winked at Jenna. He didn't care. Still staring at Jenna, he took a bite of the cake and ice cream.

CHAPTER FORTY-THREE

"OH, THIS IS delicious!" said Josiah. "I've never tasted anything like this before. What is it called?"

"This is Rocky Road ice cream—it has marshmallows and nuts in it—and this is checkerboard cake," said Jenna.

"I've never seen cake like this before," said Samuel.

Jenna looked across the table at Josiah. He was enjoying the cake, but still staring at her. It was working out perfectly—he hadn't taken his eyes off her all night.

The room stayed silent while everyone enjoyed the dessert that Jenna brought. Josiah watched her every minute as he devoured the cake and ice cream. Then he stood up to go.

"Thanks, Eliza. Thanks for the dessert, Jenna. Can you come out here to talk to me for a minute, please?"

Jenna would have felt good about that except his voice was as cold as the ice cream. Eliza gave Josiah a funny look. Samuel asked for another piece of cake.

Jenna stood up and followed Josiah out to the hotel lobby. Then she remembered that she owed him the money for the coins. "Josiah, I'll be right back," she said and then ran upstairs to retrieve the money.

Josiah stood close to the door waiting for her. He gazed out the window instead of watching her come down the stairs.

"Here's part of the money, Josiah. I could only find enough silver coins to cover six of the gold ones. But I can get the rest later. Don't worry. I'll get it all for you." She smiled up at him.

Josiah held out his hand for the money, but didn't look at her. He poked through the coins in his hand. "You don't need to cash out the rest. You can keep the money from the last three coins. Reward money."

"Okay, thanks! That's generous of you."

"Jenna, I wanted to apologize for the way I treated you last weekend. I didn't mean to be rude; there was a lot going on. I'm sorry." He kept staring at the coins in his hand and didn't look up once.

"Thanks for telling me, Josiah. I appreciate that."

"And I have to tell you something else, Jenna." His eyes never left the coins in his hand. "I wanted to ask you not to return here, but Eliza asked me not to. So I'll say it this way: I don't want to ever see you again. Ever. Good-bye." And he walked out the door without ever glancing in her direction.

Jenna watched him walk away and blinked back the tears in her eyes. Oh, Granny, she thought, this is going to be much harder than I imagined. How can I ignore that? He said he never wants to see me again. What do I do now?

Eliza came into the room and interrupted her silent conversation with her grandmother. Jenna turned to her with tears in her eyes. "What did he say to you, child?" Eliza asked.

"He said that you had asked him not to ask me to leave. But he never wants to see me again." The tears fell with abandon. Jenna couldn't stop them.

Eliza wrapped her arms around her and patted her back. "Don't worry, dear. It will all work out. That man is just bullheaded. Did you see the way he stared at you all night? He doesn't want to see you because it makes him feel things he doesn't want to feel."

"I don't know how it could possibly work out now," said Jenna.

"You said your brother and his friend are coming tomorrow?" Jenna nodded. "Well, that may just spur his interest. If not, we'll figure something else out." Eliza hesitated. "Jenna, you know that if you told him you're thinking of buying that ranch, it would probably move everything along in your favor."

"I can't do that," said Jenna, getting hold of herself. "Josiah needs to decide about me on his own. I feel that telling him I'm buying the ranch is like cheating."

"Things are certainly done differently where you come from, dear. Most women would use every trick they could think of to get their man."

Jenna shook her head. "There are still women like that where I come from, but I'm not one of them. If Josiah and I are meant to be together, he will come to me on his own, without any help."

Changing the subject, Jenna said, "I think I'm going to the saloon now to hear Sarah sing. That will cheer me up." She turned toward the door. "Oh, no, first I'll help you clean up!"

"No, child, you go on now. I can manage on my own. Samuel will help. Go on. Try to enjoy yourself and forget about that bullheaded man for now."

186

Jenna wiped away her tears, straightened her back, held her head up high, and walked across the street. She pushed through the swinging doors and chose a seat close to the piano. Noticing Josiah sitting at the bar, Jenna focused on Sarah and didn't look his way again.

The young man, Zack, came over to the table and asked if he could get her anything. She smiled and told him a sarsaparilla. When he brought it back, she handed him fifty cents and told him to keep the change. He smiled broadly and thanked her.

Jenna recognized some songs Sarah sang, like "Blue Tail Fly" and "Swanee River," but most of them she had never heard before. Or at least didn't remember ever hearing them. She took a deep breath. Josiah knew she was there. Jenna was certain of that. She had seen Matthew, the bartender, looking at her and then saying something to Josiah. But Josiah did not look at her once.

After an hour and two more sarsaparillas, Jenna wanted to leave. Although she enjoyed hearing Sarah sing, she felt there was too much tension in the room with Josiah sitting twenty feet away. And there are just so many sarsaparillas you can drink. Jenna left the saloon, crossed the street, walked upstairs, crawled into bed, and cried herself to sleep.

CHAPTER FORTY-FOUR

JENNA WOKE EARLY but didn't stir. She had nothing to get up for, anyway. Ryan, Nick, and Kat wouldn't be coming until later. And Josiah didn't want to see her, so she shouldn't even venture outside.

Wait! What would Granny do in a situation like this? She wouldn't stay inside moping. She'd go outside, parade in front of his office, and harass him. And that's exactly what Jenna intended to do. The idea made her smile. Then it made her laugh.

And that woke Sarah. "What? What's going on? Why are you laughing? Or is that the TV?"

"Sarah, you're dreaming. We're in the nineteenth century. No TV here, girlfriend."

Sarah stretched her arms and yawned. "I had a great night last night! You know, I think I could do that every night and never tire of it."

"Maybe you could buy a ranch here, too," said Jenna.

"No, no, I'm not going that far. I still like my modern conveniences." She reached for her cell phone to check her messages.

"You can't receive messages here! Why do you keep

checking?"

"Just in case. You never know!"

"Sarah, it's impossible. There are no satellites now. No cell towers. It's impossible."

"Some would say that about visiting the nineteenth century," said Sarah.

Jenna laughed. "Good point!"

"So what were you laughing about? I hope you woke me up with good reason."

"I decided I'm going to put on my other beautiful dress and parade up and down in front of Josiah's office." Although Jenna normally didn't want to wear a new dress in the saddle, some things were more important than other things. Today, she would do just that.

"Why would you do that? Aren't you going to have dinner—I mean supper—with him tonight?"

"No. Josiah told me that he never wants to see me again. He would have asked me to leave and not come back, but Eliza wouldn't let him."

"And Granny said to ignore him when he said anything like that," said Sarah.

"But this is even better. I'm sure Granny would approve. So, let's get up and have breakfast, and then I'll go do my parading. I'm so looking forward to this!"

The two women got dressed and enjoyed another breakfast in the restaurant, served by Eliza. "When is your brother coming to town, Jenna?"

"He'll be here a little later."

"You be sure to bring him around. I'd love to meet him!"

"Okay, I'll bring them all over after we see the ranch."

"Any interesting plans before they get here?"

"Yes!" said Jenna, smiling. "Since Josiah said he

doesn't want to see me, I'm going to make sure he does!"

Eliza laughed and clapped her hands. "Good for you! Make him miserable until he comes to his senses!" She walked off still laughing.

Sarah and Jenna finished breakfast and walked outside into the sunlight. "Do you want to parade around with me?" asked Jenna.

"No, I'm going to hang out at the saloon."

"You spend lots of time there even when you're not singing. Is anything going on that I should know about?"

"No, I'm just getting to know people and trying to fit in. I sometimes feel like *A Connecticut Yankee in King Arthur's Court*. But most of the time, people are people, no matter what century it is."

"Have you talked to that sweetheart of a young man, Zack?"

"Yes, he is a sweetheart. They usually call him 'Chief.'"

"Why do they call him that?"

"His parents are both gone now, but his mother was Native American."

"That's terrible to call him that."

Sarah frowned. "That's one of the nicer names they call him."

"Oh, poor kid."

"Zack lives upstairs. Matthew took him in years ago when his father died."

"Matthew's a good guy."

"Yes, he is," agreed Sarah. "Well, I have to go. Enjoy your parading!"

Jenna smiled at her friend, lifted her head in an arrogant posture, and walked toward Josiah's office. She looked in the window and saw him sitting at his desk staring off into space. Tapping at the window, she smiled when he looked up, and then she waved. He scowled at her.

Then she walked to the end of the block past the general store, turned around, and walked back in front of his window. Then she did it again. And again. And again. She'd do it until she got a response, even if she had to walk back and forth until Ryan, Nick, and Kat showed up.

But she didn't have to wait long. Josiah burst out of his office with eyebrows knitted and mouth drawn tight. "What do you think you're doing? I told you I didn't want to see you anymore!"

With her chin held high, she looked him right in the eye. "I could be wrong, but if I recall my history correctly, this was a free country in 1870. And you, Josiah Stone, are not the boss of me. It's a public street, and I can walk on it if I want to walk on it."

"I told you, I don't want to look at you!"

"Why not, Josiah? What's wrong with me?" Jenna stepped away from him and twirled around.

When Jenna turned back, she saw that his expression had softened. He looked her up and down, shook his head, and walked back into his office. When she glanced in there, he was still staring at her. Mission accomplished, thought Jenna.

Since it was getting close to when Ryan and the others would arrive, she walked over to the livery stable to get Magic. She waited while Ezra saddled him for her, and then she walked him over and dropped his reins over the hitching post in front of Josiah's office. When the others saw her horse, they would stop there, and that would be perfect.

Jenna walked over to the saloon, thinking she could kill some time with Sarah. But as she stood at the swinging doors before entering, she saw that Sarah was in a serious conversation with Matthew and Zack. She decided she'd walk around while she waited.

CHAPTER FORTY-FIVE

JENNA HAD ROUNDED the corner by the doctor's office when she saw Ryan, Nick, and Kat ride into town. They used the hitching post in front of Josiah's office, like she hoped they would. As she walked by, she quickly looked in his window to see if he was watching, and he was. So she made a big deal of hugging Ryan and Nick, and then she hugged Kat as well.

She had already told Ryan not to mention the ranch in front of the sheriff, so she hoped that he had noticed he was standing in front of that office right now. "Do you want me to show you around the town first, or just go —?" asked Jenna.

Ryan looked into the office, put his arm around her, and said, "Let's go first and relax later. Okay with you?"

"Perfect," said Jenna.

Jenna climbed into the saddle with the help of Nick. Her long dress kept getting in the way. The others mounted their horses, and Jenna led the way back the way they had come.

Once they reached the outskirts of town, Nick and Kat, who hadn't heard the whole story, bombarded her with questions about how she had discovered the cave and how much time she had already spent here. They loved the story of Hilary Clinton, and they were looking forward to meeting Eliza and Samuel. She didn't go into details about Josiah. Ryan already knew, and he would tell Kat later. But they all knew not to mention the ranch in front of him.

Then they reached the ranch. It was set back from the road, which Jenna liked. Although the ranch was on a hundred-acre parcel, there were no fences. She'd need at least one pasture fenced for her horses. And she wanted the barn to have the same setup as the one back in *their* Red Bluff, so the horses could get out in case of fire.

"Can you do that, Ryan?"

"Jenna, just because that barn burned down, doesn't mean every barn is going to burn down."

"Ryan," said Kat, "her request is perfectly under-standable. Can you do it or not?" Kat was Ryan and Jenna's older sister, and the voice of reason.

"I'd have to look at the barn, but I'm sure I could work something out. We might have to hire Nick to help me."

The small group dismounted in front of the barn. Nick and Ryan walked inside and looked around. A horse, munching hay, stood in one stall. And his harness hung on the next stall. In the center of the barn was a horse-drawn wagon. Then they examined the outside walls of the barn.

"It's built really well, Jenna," said Ryan. "If the house is in as good a condition as the barn, then you're good to go."

"Cool," said Jenna. Then, covering her mouth, she said, "I haven't said that in a month!" Everyone laughed.

"Let's go inside now, but don't talk about the changes I want. It might make Annie suspicious."

"Why is there so much secrecy involved here, Jenna? Are you hiding something?" asked Nick.

Nick could be annoying at times, and Jenna wasn't in the mood for his antics. "Yes, Nick, I'm trying to hide something. I'm trying to hide the little detail that I come from a different century!"

He put his hands out in front of him as if to ward her off. "Okay, okay, I see your point."

They came through the trees, and the house appeared. Kat gasped. "Ooooh, it's beautiful! I never expected this!"

Nick laughed. "I bet you were expecting something old, something that looked like it was from the 1800s—a couple of centuries old! All those old log houses were once new—like this one. It is beautiful."

"But it's not made out of logs," said Kat.

"These are rough-hewn logs, Kat," said Ryan. "The bark has been removed and the logs have been hand-hewn. It's really pretty awesome! Jenna, this is a find! If you don't buy it, I will!"

Walking up the curving path toward the house, Jenna loved how the house was surrounded by trees. And the split rail fence in front of the house made it so cute—almost like a doll house. And it was about to be hers!

CHAPTER FORTY-SIX

JOSIAH STOMPED AROUND his office swearing to himself. That dratted woman! She was just piling on the agony! How dare she go parading around right outside his office after he had told her he didn't want to see her again! She said he wasn't the boss of her! What did that even mean? He couldn't get over how she did that deliberately to taunt him. Especially after what he had said to her.

He nodded his head. Jenna had nerve. Josiah liked that in a woman. She had stood up to him. Most people around Red Bluff honored and respected him. They would never do that. Jenna did. And she had on another beautiful dress, even more beautiful than yesterday's. She was trying to kill him. That was it. She wanted to kill him.

Because he couldn't go on tortured like this. He wouldn't. Of course, what could he do if she continued doing whatever she pleased? Would he leave town? That was just stupid. He could get over this. Get over her. She's just a woman. She had no hold on him.

Who were those new people who came into town? Those two men got awfully friendly with her. Josiah didn't like that at all. Dang it! He had such contradictory thoughts in his head. He wanted her, he didn't want her. He didn't want to look at her, he couldn't stop looking at her. There was one thought in his head that he was sure about. It would never work out with two people from different centuries. The whole idea of it was absurd. What did she want him to do? Move into her century? He didn't think so! He loved it here. This is where he always wanted to be, out west. That's why he moved here from Boston.

Josiah decided that he needed some fresh air. He walked out of his office and strode over to the livery. After Ezra saddled his horse for him, Josiah mounted up and rode out of town. The way Jenna and her friends went. It was a free country, like she said. He could go this way if he wanted to.

Where'd they go? Jenna didn't have her bag attached to her saddle, so he didn't think she had left town. Did they go back through the cave? Since he didn't have anything else to do, he might as well check it out. Because he was curious. That's all.

There were horse tracks leading out from the cave, but not back in. So Jenna's friends didn't return to their own century. Where else would they go? Back on the main road, Josiah continued heading out of town.

I'm not looking for them, he thought. I'm a free man out for a ride. She can do what she wants. He was through with her. Even if she was beautiful. Even if she had nerve enough to walk in front of his office. What kind of a wife would she make if she wouldn't even listen to him? Wife? What was he thinking? He needed to get her off his mind. Then why was he following her and her friends now?

He changed his mind. Josiah reined in Patches and turned him back toward town. No. He didn't want to do that, either. Turning Patches back around the other way, he motioned for the horse to go forward again. Maybe he'd go look at Annie's ranch. Although he had never been there, he had heard that it had a comfortable ranch house and a good size barn. And Annie would probably sell it to him for not much money.

Josiah turned Patches around again. What was he thinking? Without a deputy, he couldn't even consider buying a ranch. And there was nobody around who even had the slightest possibility of fitting that job. He was stuck with a woman who tortured him and no deputy. If it wasn't so funny, he'd have to cry. Laughing to himself, Josiah returned to town.

CHAPTER FORTY-SEVEN

JENNA KNOCKED ON the front door. When the door opened, Annie stood in the doorway and looked at them blankly.

"Hello, Annie! We've come to look at the house again, if you don't mind."

The door swung slowly open. "No, I don't mind. Come in."

They walked into a large open room. To the right side of the door was a large container filled with firewood. Beyond the wood container was the kitchen. It had cabinets holding dishes and cooking utensils. In the center of the room stood a large wood cooking stove. A metal bathtub was on the floor close to the wood stove. Ryan and Nick examined the door they had just passed through. Then they walked around the room, examining the walls, the windows, and the floor. The windows had glass in them, but the glass was an inferior quality and distorted everything you saw.

Two doors opened off the main room. Ryan and Nick walked into one bedroom while Jenna and Kat stood in the doorway. The bedroom had its own small wood stove. The second doorway led to another bedroom with another small wood stove. When Ryan and Nick emerged from the second bedroom, Ryan nodded to Jenna.

"It's solid and in good shape, Jenna."

Kat faced Annie. "Annie, how do you get upstairs?"

Annie looked at her blankly. "There is no upstairs."

"There's an upstairs window, which indicates an up-stairs!" Kat didn't like to be contradicted. Jenna smiled to herself at Kat's reaction. But she had also noticed the upstairs window and wanted to know about the upstairs, too.

"Oh, yeah. There's an attic." Annie pushed into the second bedroom and pointed to a trap door in the ceiling.

Kat glanced at the ceiling. "And Annie, do you have a root cellar?"

Without answering, Annie moved to the kitchen window and pointed. "Right there, between the house and the barn."

"What difference does it make, Kat?"

"The root cellar will keep your food cold, Jenna. Ryan, Nick, let's go look at the root cellar." The two men followed Kat outside, while Jenna remained inside.

"So, Annie, I like it. I'm interested in buying it. How much are you asking?" Jenna had no idea how much a ranch house, barn, and one hundred acres would cost. But considering the cost of everything else she had encountered, she didn't think it would be expensive.

Annie looked at her, still with that bland expression in her face. "I was hoping to get two thousand dollars."

Jenna tried not to look surprised. She could pay for it with the money she'd get from cashing in the three gold coins that she received for helping to catch Hilary Clinton. "Oh, well, yeah, I think I can handle that. I'll take it." Jenna held out her hand to Annie, and Annie stared at it. Quickly, Jenna drew it back to her side. She had forgotten that women didn't shake hands in the nineteenth century.

"How soon do you want it?" asked Annie.

"Whenever you're willing to part with it."

"I need to talk to Sheriff Josiah and make sure that man Rawlins is out of the house I'll be living in. The one across from the school."

"Don't ask the sheriff today." Jenna didn't want Josiah to get any clue that she was the buyer. "Next week is fine. How long will it take you to move out once that other house is vacant?"

"I don't have that many clothes," said Annie.

"What about all the furniture?" She looked around. Some of it looked really cool. All antiques of course. Except they weren't. Most of it was in perfect condition.

"Would you like to buy any of it? I'm moving into a furnished house. So you could have it all, if you wanted."

Jenna looked around the room. There were a sofa and chairs at the far side of the room. A table was at either end of the sofa. A wooden secretary stood against one wall. The top was down, and there were paper and a quill pen on top of it. When the top was up, it hid the many compartments above. Two bookcases, filled with books, were against another wall. Beside the big cabinet in the kitchen stood another smaller, narrow cabinet with a decorated metal front.

Stepping back into the bedrooms, Jenna saw that each had a small double bed and a dresser, and one room had an old chifforobe. Perfect. She loved chifforobes, thought they were beautiful, and had always wanted one.

Jenna walked back to the living area of the house. She thought about what she was paying for the entire ranch and said, "I'll give you twenty-five dollars for all the furniture in the house."

"Fine," said Annie.

"I'll check back, on Wednesday, to see if you're ready. Is that all right?"

"Yes. That sounds perfect. Good-bye." And with that, Annie walked to the door and opened it for Jenna.

"Good-bye, Annie, thank you." When she stepped away from the house, Jenna smiled at Annie's discomfort. She thought that Annie would be a great match with the storekeeper, Henry Ralston. He wouldn't shut up, and she hardly said a word.

CHAPTER FORTY-EIGHT

Ryan, Nick, and Kat couldn't stop talking about Jenna buying the hundred-acre ranch for two thousand dollars *and* a house full of antiques for only twenty-five dollars.

"Easy, guys, easy. They're not considered antiques back in this time," said Jenna. "Some of that stuff is nearly new."

"Still, Jenna," said Ryan, "that is an awesome deal. I hope this cowboy of yours comes around so you can enjoy it."

"I can enjoy it without the cowboy," said Jenna indignantly.

"Yes, but you'd enjoy it a lot more with the cowboy!" said Kat.

Everyone laughed, including Jenna, and then they talked about all the changes Jenna wanted made to the property. Besides building a fence surrounding the pasture and the changes to the barn, the house would need some adjustments as well.

"How difficult would it be to bring back window glass from our time?" asked Jenna. "I would hate looking out those distorted windows."

"On horseback? Very difficult," said Nick.

"But I can do that if it's what you want," said Ryan. "It's going to cost you, though. You know you'll have to pay me with twenty-first-century prices!" He grinned at her. "I can do everything you ask, but it'll cost ya!"

"When will you do it, Ryan? Do you have someone to look after the store for you?" asked Kat.

"No, I'm selling the store. I have two or three people looking at it and considering it right now. I've put it up for a reasonable price, so I know it will sell quickly."

"Then what will you do?" asked Kat.

"Jenna's work, for starters. After that, I know the right thing will come along for me. I want something that gives me the time to paint—which is what I want to do, anyway."

"Back to the house," said Jenna. "Is there a way you can build a passageway to the outhouse, so I don't have to walk through the snow in the winter?"

"Outhouses need to be moved regularly, Jenna," said Nick.

"That's true," said Ryan. "Maybe I can make a passageway with hinges, so it could move with the outhouse."

"What's wrong with an indoor bathroom?" asked Kat.

"There's no indoor plumbing for a few more years, I think," said Jenna.

"I have an idea where you wouldn't need indoor plumbing. How about a composting toilet? It would be perfect. Then you wouldn't have to go outside at all!"

"Ryan, is it possible?"

"I know nothing about composting toilets, but I'll check it out for you. Then I'd have to build you a room to put it in. That wouldn't be a problem, either. Great idea, Kat!"

When they reached the signpost for Red Bluff, Jenna encouraged them to stop talking about the house. "When are you going back?" she asked.

"We didn't plan to stay too long," said Ryan.

"I would like you to meet Eliza before you go," said Jenna.

When Ryan guided his horse to the hitching post in front of the sheriff's office, Jenna said, "No, over here," and she crossed the street and dismounted in front of the hotel. To Kat, she whispered, "No use torturing the man too much!"

CHAPTER FORTY-NINE

WHEN THEY WALKED into the hotel, Eliza and her father, Edward, greeted them. After all the introductions, Ryan noticed the pictures on the wall. "Who did these?" he asked. "They're gorgeous."

"That would be me," said Edward. "I don't know about gorgeous, but I don't think they're too bad for an old fart!"

"Dad!" said Eliza, embarrassed.

"Eliza, I am seventy-three years old, and I can say whatever I want!" said Edward.

"He sounds like my grandmother!" said Jenna.

"Oh, no," complained Eliza, joking, "not two of them." She pretended to hit her head with her palm.

"Do you have any more?" Ryan asked Edward.

"They're all over the hotel and in some rooms. Too bad I can't paint anymore. I miss my painting."

"Why can't you paint anymore?" asked Ryan.

"No paints. I've tried, and they're not available or something. Henry at the general store has tried and tried," said Edward.

Ryan winked at him. "I can probably solve that problem for you."

"Ryan," Nick interrupted. "I know you want to look at the paintings, but how about we go over to the saloon for a quick beer?"

"Good idea," said Ryan. "Nice meeting you, Eliza, Edward. I'll see you again." Then he followed Nick outside and across the street.

Edward wandered over to the window. Eliza said to Kat, "So you live in the same place that Jenna does?"

"Yes, we all do. Red—um, yes." Jenna noticed that Kat realized too late not to mention the town.

"Ah, still the mystery," said Eliza and smiled. "Well, it doesn't matter to us where Jenna comes from. We've come to love her." She put one arm around Jenna and pulled her into a fond embrace.

Suddenly, Edward erupted into laughter. "Oh, that Josiah! He's at it again!"

Eliza glanced out the window, then at Jenna, and said, "Oh, no. Not again."

"Let's go outside and watch!" said Edward.

"No, I don't think we should," said Eliza.

By that time, Jenna had looked out the window. "Come on, Kat." She grabbed her sister's arm and pulled her out the door behind Edward. Eliza followed.

A crowd had gathered in front of the saloon, including her brother Ryan and his friend Nick. Two men faced each other in the street, their arms in a "ready-to-shoot" stance. Jenna watched as Josiah, with his back toward her, stepped between the two men.

"Don't worry, he'll be fine," she whispered to Kat.

Josiah put his arms out and said loudly, "Settle down, gentlemen. There are other ways to settle this."

Then a shot rang out. The man at the far end of the

207

street had drawn his gun and fired. Josiah staggered and fell to the ground. The other man started to draw his gun. Nick, a cop in the *other* Red Bluff, saw what was happening and jumped the man before the gun came out of the holster. Knocking him down, Nick wrestled the gun away from him.

When she heard the shot and saw Josiah fall, Jenna screamed, "Oh no!" and ran to Josiah. She knelt down, put her arms around his neck, and hugged Josiah

Kat followed her out there. "Move over, Jenna," she commanded. Kat, a nurse practitioner, was on the other side of Josiah. "It's just a flesh wound. He'll be fine. Is there a doctor here in town?"

"No, no," said Josiah. "I still have work to do."

Nick, holding a gun in one hand and holding the man's arm behind his back with the other, said, "What do you want me to do with this guy and the other one, Sheriff?"

"Run them out of town!" said Josiah. "And then go to the saloon and get rid of anyone who rode in with them. I don't need their kind in my town." Josiah moaned and wanted to hold his arm, but Kat pushed his hand away.

"Don't touch it, Sheriff," she said.

"Hey," Josiah said to Nick. "You're a good man. You wanna be a deputy?"

"Sure thing!" Nick smiled and led the two men away, still holding the gun on them.

Kat said, "I need some men who will help carry him to the doctor's office." She had taken Josiah's kerchief off his neck, wrapped it around his arm, and held it tight.

"Nonsense," said Josiah. "I can walk. Help me up."

All this time, Jenna was clinging to him and crying.

208

But now she helped him rise to his feet.

"You're a tough one, aren't you, Sheriff?" said Kat. "Where's the doctor's office?"

"This way," said Jenna. "Oh, Josiah, meet my sister, Kat. Kat, this is Josiah."

"Nice meeting you, Kat. You seem to know what you're doing."

"I'm a nurse, Josiah," said Kat.

"Here we are," said Jenna. She opened the door and called out for the doctor.

CHAPTER FIFTY

DOC CAME RUNNING down the stairs. "Josiah? Are you up to your old tricks again? Come on, let's get you in here." The doctor led the way into a room with a long, narrow table.

Josiah boosted himself up on the table with his right arm. "Doc Mercer, this is Jenna Leyton and Kat somebody. Kat knows what she's doing."

"Good to know, Josiah." Doc Mercer nodded toward the two women and tore the shirt off Josiah's arm.

"Doc, no offense, but before you start could you wash your hands?"

"Why?" asked Doc.

Kat put her hands on her hips. "Because I'm from the future, and washing your hands stops the spread of disease!"

Doc laughed. "And I'm from the moon!"

Kat pushed in front of Doc Mercer and blocked his path to Josiah's arm. "I'm serious. About washing your hands. Do it, or I won't let you touch him."

"Fine, fine," said Doc. He brought a bowl of water and a bar of soap into the room. Scrubbing his hands, he said, "Does this make you feel better, Kat?"

"Yes, it does," she said. Then she walked over to the bowl and washed her hands.

Back by Josiah's arm, Doc said, "Oh, bad news, Josiah. The bullet didn't go all the way through. I'm going to have to take it out."

Eliza walked in the door then. "Is that rascal all right? I knew this would eventually happen if he kept up those antics."

"Eliza," said Doc Mercer. "The rascal will be fine, but I need to take the bullet out. Can you go to the saloon and get a bottle of whiskey? Josiah's going to need it." Eliza hurried back out the door.

"I don't drink when I'm on the job, Doc. You know that," said Josiah.

"You are officially off the job, right now," said Doc.

Jenna clung to Josiah's good arm and felt grateful that he didn't tell her to leave. "I'm glad you're okay, Josiah."

"Thanks, Jenna, I'm glad you're here. Thank you."

Eliza rushed back into the room with the bottle. "Here you go." She handed it to Kat.

"Doc, I know you will think this is crazy, but how about boiling some water to clean your instruments before you begin?" asked Kat.

"Boil my instruments? Now I *know* you're crazy as a loon! I will not let you ruin my instruments by putting them in hot water! No! Absolutely not!"

Resigned, Kat sighed and said, "Okay, pour Josiah as much whiskey as you need to, but save enough to clean your instruments," said Kat.

"Wash my hands *and* clean my instruments? Honestly, Kat, whoever you are, this is ridiculous."

She stood in front of Josiah's arm. "Do it or I won't let

211

you touch him."

Josiah whispered to Jenna, although everyone could hear, "Jenna, what's your sister doing?"

Jenna whispered back, although everyone could still hear, "She's a nurse, Josiah."

"From—?" he asked.

"Yes," said Jenna.

"Doc, I don't know what's going on, but put your instruments in the whiskey," Josiah said. "It's not a big deal, right?"

"I'll do it because you're telling me, too, Josiah, but I think this is absurd." Doc disappeared into the other room and came back with a large bowl and a cup. He poured some whiskey in the cup for Josiah. While Josiah drank it, he put the instruments he planned to use into the bowl. When Josiah finished drinking the whiskey, Doc poured him more.

"I'm not a whiskey man, Doc. How much of this do I have to drink?"

"This is going to hurt, Josiah. You'd better drink it down."

Josiah drank it all in one gulp and held out the cup for more. "I think I'll have some more," said Josiah, but it didn't sound like his voice.

"I think one more will do it, Josiah," said Doc. He poured Josiah another full cup of whiskey and poured the rest of the bottle into the bowl with the instruments.

When Josiah finished, Doc asked him to lie down on the table, which Josiah willingly did. Jenna held his hand the whole time, and Josiah didn't resist.

"I suppose you're planning to help me, right?" Doc asked Kat.

"I'm right here at your side, Doctor, if you should

need me," said Kat.

"I'm feeling good right now, Doc. Can I have some more of that whiskey?"

"Sorry, Josiah, but your girlfriend here made me wash my instruments in it for some strange reason. Maybe she is from the future and knows something I don't."

"Kat's not my girlfriend, Doc. Jenna is." Josiah brought Jenna's hand up to his mouth and kissed it. "You know, Doc, she is from the future. Both of 'em. Honestly. And the two men who were with 'em, too, I'll bet."

Doc laughed. "You've had enough whiskey, Josiah. Next you'll be telling me they're from another planet!"

"Well, that's what I thought at first, Doc, but no, that's not it at all. They're from the future. *Red Bluff*'s future! I went there. They have these big things there called trucks! They're huge! You should see 'em. I'm getting tired now."

Doc picked up an instrument and asked Kat to hold Josiah's arm for him. "That's good, Josiah. This would be a good time to sleep." Doc poked around inside the bullet wound.

"You know, Doc, that hurts. Jenna, you know what? I love you. Do you know that?"

Jenna kissed his cheek and looked at Kat helplessly, but Kat was focused on Josiah's arm. "I know, Josiah. I know."

"Ouch! Did you get it, Doc?"

"Still looking, Josiah, sorry."

"Jenna, I want to say I do love you. The reason I told you not to come back here anymore is because every time I see you, I love you more. You're the best thing that's ever happened to me. I never want to be without you. Do you love me, too, my sweet Jenna?"

213

Jenna kissed his cheek. "Yes, I do, Josiah. I love you, too. With all my heart."

"Oh, good, then if Doc kills me I can go to my grave knowing you love me. Good night." And he fell asleep on the table.

CHAPTER FIFTY-ONE

"AH, GOT IT," said Doc. He dropped the bullet and the instrument into the bowl of whiskey.

"Good job!" said Kat.

"You think so?" asked Doc. "Even for an old country doctor?"

Kat laughed. "Even for a twenty-first-century doctor. If it wasn't for dirty hands and dirty instruments, you'd be all right."

Doc smiled and bowed. "Well, thank you, sweet lady from the future!" Doc bandaged Josiah's wound with Kat looking on.

Then Doc and Kat looked at Jenna, who was holding Josiah's limp hand and looking at him lovingly. She looked up when she felt their stares on her. "He'll be okay, right?"

"He'll be fine, little lady. I hate to be the bearer of bad news, but he was drunk when he said those things to you. He might say something different when he sobers up."

Jenna sighed. "I know. But it was good to hear, regardless."

"Jenna, he'll probably be out for a while. The boys are

215

probably waiting for me. We need to get going."

As if on cue, the door opened, and Ryan and Nick walked in. "Is he all right?" asked Ryan.

"Yes, he'll be fine after he sleeps this off," said Doc. "He'll have a sore arm for a while, but it will heal."

"Kat, we need to skedaddle out of here," said Nick. "I didn't think we'd be staying this long."

"Yeah, I figured you'd be ready to go. I'm ready. I've butted my nose in enough here," said Kat.

"Jenna?" asked Ryan.

"Oh, I'm staying, Ryan. I'm having dinner with Eliza tonight."

"See you at home, then."

The two men walked out. Kat turned around at the door and said, "Jenna, he'll be out for a while. You might as well let him sleep it off."

"Okay, Kat, thanks for helping." She kissed Josiah's cheek and said, "Thank you, Doc." Then she walked to the door, hugged Kat, and said, "Thanks for everything, Kat. I love you."

"Love you, too, Sis. See you later."

As Kat walked through the door, Sarah walked in. She glanced into the other room and saw Josiah lying limp on the table. "Is he dead, Jenna? I'm so sorry!" she said and hugged Jenna.

"Thanks for the hug, Sarah, but he'll be fine. It was just a flesh wound in his arm."

"Oh thank goodness!" said Sarah. "I was in the out-house when it happened," she whispered to Jenna. "I heard the shot, though, and heard that the sheriff had been shot and Doc was operating on him. I didn't want to come in and disturb anything. Then I saw the boys leave, so I came in. He'll be all right, then?"

"Let's go," said Jenna. "Thanks, Doc," she called behind her as she led Sarah out the door. "Josiah told me he loved me. He said I was the best thing that had ever happened to him, and he never wanted to be without me."

"Jenna, that's great!"

Jenna frowned. "Well, not exactly. He was drunk at the time."

"He still said it and meant it, though."

"Although he may have meant it, it doesn't mean he'll want me around when he sobers up. He still has issues with me being from the future," she sighed. "Oh, that reminds me. I bought the ranch! Two thousand dollars for a ranch with a hundred acres!"

"Yeah, but does it have an indoor bathroom?"

"Not now, but it will! Kat came up with the brilliant idea to put in a composting toilet."

"Now all you have to do is tell the big guy back there that you're moving into town, and he'll be fine."

"I don't want him like that," said Jenna.

"What do you mean?"

"I want him to want me without knowing that I purchased the ranch. Everybody who knows about the ranch is sworn to secrecy. I know it's silly, but I feel strongly about this."

"Okay, well, you know you can count on me." They had arrived at the entrance to the saloon. "When do you have to go to dinner?"

"Supper," Jenna corrected. "Not for a couple of hours."

"Come on in and let's talk before you have to go."

They walked into the saloon and sat at a table near the piano. Several people came over asking Jenna how the sheriff was doing. She gave them a full report, and then she and Sarah talked about this and that for the next hour.

"Sarah, I need to talk to Eliza."

"Why?"

"I don't know, I just do. I'll tell her that Josiah is fine, and after that, I don't know. So, I'll see you later, or tomorrow morning. Bye."

"Bye, Jenna, enjoy your dinner. I mean supper!"

CHAPTER FIFTY-TWO

JENNA WALKED OUT of the saloon and looked down the street. She wondered if she should go check on Josiah. No, he was at the doctor's office and probably still sleeping it off. She crossed the street to the hotel, opened the door, and saw Eliza working behind the front desk.

"Hi, Eliza. Josiah's fine. The doctor took out the bullet."

"I'm glad to hear that. Jenna, can you come with me into my sitting room, please?"

Jenna took a deep breath. Eliza's voice didn't sound right. Maybe she was just worried about Josiah.

"Sure, Eliza." She followed the woman into the other room.

"Sit here with me, Jenna. Across from me. So, I can see your eyes."

"See my eyes?" asked Jenna.

"It's time for the truth, Jenna." Jenna raised her eyebrows, but didn't say a word. "I was standing next to you during the failed gunfight, and I heard you say to your sister, 'Don't worry, he'll be fine.' And he is fine. But it surprised you when he got shot. I'm feeling all-overish—

uncomfortable—about this. I don't understand this, and I want to. Please, Jenna, talk to me."

Jenna looked down and took a deep breath. How would she tell this kindly woman, whose friendship she valued, the truth so she would believe her? Just do it, I guess. She looked into Eliza's eyes.

"Eliza, your friendship is important to me."

"And your friendship is important to me, too, Jenna. I've already told you that I've grown fond of you."

"Eliza, I come from the future. I come from a twenty-first-century version of Red Bluff."

Eliza looked at her and didn't blink. "Go on."

"You *believe* me?" asked Jenna.

"Yes, child. I knew there was something odd about you, but I couldn't put my finger on it. And the cake and ice cream you brought—and that container. Strange things that don't belong in this time. But how did you know nothing would happen to Josiah?"

"Well, I knew he wouldn't die. But it scared me so much because I had no idea that he would get shot."

"*How* did you know that he wouldn't die?"

Jenna blinked her eyes and took another deep breath. "You told me that before I got involved with him I should give it some consideration because he might be killed. So when I got home—to the future—I looked it up. You know, when he died. That's how I knew he wouldn't be killed today. But I didn't realize there might be a chance that he'd get shot and not killed. I never considered that." Jenna thought that if she was going to tell Eliza about her son Brian being alive, that now would be a good time. But she decided against it.

Eliza's eyes glittered. "Tell me more about this future of yours."

Jenna spent the next hour telling her all about the future. Eliza was a rapt listener and kept encouraging Jenna to go on. Jenna started with the story about Hilary Clinton, and then told her everything from cars and planes to computers and skyscrapers to cities and wars.

"While you two women are sitting around gabbing, who's cooking supper?" Edward, Eliza's father, had stepped into the room.

"Oh, Dad, I forgot all about supper! Jenna was telling me the most fascinating story."

"Well, you'll have to share it with me later. Right now, I'll go in the back into the kitchen and throw something together. You two go on talking. I don't want to disturb a good story. Where's Sam?"

"He's cooking in the restaurant," said Eliza. "I should go help you, Dad."

"No such thing! You stay out here and keep gabbing. I'll be fine," said Edward.

"Jenna, this is fascinating! I want to hear more, but I should go help my dad."

Jenna smiled and nodded. She watched Eliza walk into the kitchen. Suddenly, Eliza was back, sitting in front of her, and taking her hands.

"Jenna, I want to experience the elephant!"

"You want to what?"

"I want to go! I want to see it all and experience it all! Josiah went! I want to go, too!"

"Oh, Eliza," Jenna shook her head. She had never expected the older woman to want to go with her to the future.

"Jenna, Josiah went, and I want to go, too!"

"Josiah went, and now he won't speak to me," said Jenna. "I don't want to lose you, too."

221

"You won't lose me, and you haven't lost him, either. Jenna, I've made up my mind. I have to see some of what you told me about. I have to!"

Jenna smiled. "Are you available Wednesday? I'm coming back on Wednesday to give Annie the—" she changed her voice to a whisper, "money for the ranch."

"Wednesday's perfect. What do I need to do? To bring?"

"Well, you need to ride a horse—"

"Oh! A horse! I haven't been on a horse for years, but I was quite the rider when I was young. I can rent one from the livery stable. No problem."

"And, Eliza, why don't you bring a dollar gold piece?"

"You're going to charge me?" Eliza joked.

"No, it's for you. But you'll be surprised what you can do with it in the future."

Eliza smiled and walked back into the kitchen to help her father. A few minutes later she came out with a platter of cold meat and freshly baked bread. "I already had the bread ready!" she said.

The three of them sat down at the table, as Samuel was still cooking for the restaurant. Eliza's dad sat across from Jenna.

"So, Jenna, where are ya from?"

"Um, from away."

"You are the secretive one, aren't you? Well, I'm not going to let you get away with it, young lady! How far away?" he demanded.

Jenna laughed and choked on her sandwich. "Farther than you can imagine, Edward. And you, you're from Pennsylvania, too?"

"Yes, my wife, Eve, talked me into coming out west and buying this hotel. Then she upped and died on me, the old biddie!"

"Dad!" said Eliza.

"Yes, yes, I know, it's your mother, and I should have more respect. I loved the woman with all my heart, but if I had died on her first, she would have said the same about me! That's what I loved about her. And you know that, too, Eliza." He patted her hand, and she nodded.

"So, Jenna, does your brother come from wherever you come from, too?"

"Yes," said Jenna hesitantly.

"I'm wondering what he meant when he said he could get me some oil paints. Nobody around here can get them. How can he?"

Jenna thought the truth—or at least part of it—would be safe. "He owns an art store."

"A whole store with just art supplies in it? I'd like to see that, sometime!"

Eliza looked at Jenna and smiled. Jenna shook her head, no. She'd take Eliza to the future, but not her father, too.

The rest of the conversation was about what happened to Josiah. Jenna had to give all the details about Josiah getting drunk, and the doctor removing the bullet. Then Edward told stories of other times that Josiah had stood in front of two men wanting a shoot out. Although this was the first time that someone had hit him, it wasn't the first time a gun was fired as Josiah stood in the middle. Edward was funny, and Jenna enjoyed the evening.

The rest of the ice cream was only slightly solid, but still delicious, and there was plenty of cake left. Edward couldn't get over the little squares of chocolate and white.

"This is amazing, Jenna! Can you get more of this?

Eliza, we need to keep this girl around! I'm going to have a talk with Josiah about this! He can't let someone like Jenna get away!"

Jenna thought the more people who were on her side, the better. She smiled at Edward and continued eating her ice cream and cake. When they finished, Edward amused her with other stories about the area and about the two times the hotel had burned down. Finally, it was time to go to sleep.

She thanked Edward and Eliza, and gave Eliza a big hug. Edward stepped around the table and hugged Jenna, too.

"You're quite the girl, Jenna. Josiah is an idiot if he doesn't snatch you right up," said Edward. "And I'm going to tell him so! Good night!"

Eliza walked Jenna to the door. "I'll see you Wednesday, Jenna. I think we should keep this a secret, don't you?"

"I was about to ask you to do that."

"I won't even tell Samuel and especially not my dad! He'd have it all over town in an instant!"

Jenna hugged Eliza again. "I'll see you tomorrow morning for breakfast and then Wednesday morning."

"Oh, good," said Eliza. "If we go in the morning, I can spend all day there! If that's okay with you, Jenna."

Jenna smiled at the older woman and walked upstairs with Josiah on her mind. She wasn't excited or thrilled with what he had said to her because she knew he was drunk when he said it. She expected him to deny all of it as soon as he sobered up, but still, it was nice to hear. Someday, she hoped to hear those words again—when he was sober.

CHAPTER FIFTY-THREE

JOSIAH FELT GRUMPY. He was back at his office sitting at his desk. His arm hurt, and he felt angry with himself. Doc had told him what he had said to Jenna, although Josiah had a vague recollection of it. Now the dratted woman would probably want something of him; something that he couldn't give. All *he* wanted was for her to go away and leave his heart alone.

The memory of her kiss, those soft, sweet lips on his, was finally beginning to fade. And he felt certain he could overcome his feelings for her if he didn't have to see her. Two people who lived in two different centuries could not be together. He slammed his fist on the desk and cried out. The motion had hurt his sore arm.

"Dang it!" he shouted at himself and was so angry that he almost hit the desk again, barely catching himself as his fist went downward. Maybe he could follow Rawlins' lead and drink her out of his system. That would work, he thought, but what would become of Josiah Stone? Because Josiah Stone was not a drunk.

See what she was doing to him! She was turning him into something he was not! He was not a drunk and had no desire or intention of becoming one because of her! She needed to go back where she came from. Then he would be fine.

He looked up. And here she was right now. Probably come to declare her undying love for him. Just what he needed to hear. Closing his eyes, he tilted his head down and willed her to walk on by.

The door opened. He looked up. Jenna walked in with a slight smile on her face.

"Hi, Josiah. I came to see how you are."

"I'm fine, thank you."

"Does it still hurt?" she asked, stepping close to the desk and looking at his sling.

"A little. But it's not bad." Taken off guard by her casual friendliness when he expected something different, he was casual back to her.

"Okay, Josiah. Sarah and I are going back to Red Bluff now—*our* Red Bluff—and I wanted to stop in to see how you were doing. And to do this," she quickly leaned over and kissed him on the mouth, lingering just long enough to see if he pulled away. He didn't.

Jenna stepped toward the door, opened it, smiled at the surprised look on his face, and walked out, saying "good-bye" before she closed the door behind her.

"That dratted woman!" shouted Josiah, slamming his fist down on the desk again and crying out in pain when it hit. "Look what she's making me do!" Settling down and cradling his injured arm, he thought that he'd have to forget that kiss all over again. He chided himself for not having the willpower to pull away.

Looking out the window, he watched as Jenna and Sarah rode away. He had to admit it to himself: he wanted that kiss as much as she did. And he also had to admit something else: he was in love with her. He was heels over head in love with her. Wondering when she might be back, he stood up and leaned into the window to see her. But they had already disappeared down the street. Josiah wondered if the love between him and Jenna was meant to be. If so, then it was useless to fight it.

Then the door of his office burst open, and Edward stood there glaring at him. "You dang fool, man! She's a huckleberry above a persimmon! How can you let someone like her get away?" Josiah glared back. "I'm thinking of trying to take up with her, myself, if she'll have me!"

"She doesn't want you," said Josiah glumly. "She wants me."

"Then why aren't you doing something about it, man? Marry that woman before she falls for someone else! There are plenty of other men in this town hungering for a woman like her!"

"Plenty of other men, Edward? You mean like Rawlins and you and young Zack? I don't think so."

"All I'm saying, Josiah, is that you're a fool to let her get away. I mean, did you taste that cake and ice cream that she brought? I'd marry her in a minute for that alone! But she's beautiful, too. It's a dang shame that a woman like that has to pine away for the likes of you!" At that, Edward opened the door, stomped outside, and slammed the door behind him.

Josiah thought that maybe he had it wrong all along. Edward's words reinforced his new thinking. If Jenna really loved him, maybe she would be willing to give up the cars and trucks and whatever else they had in her century and come live with him. But where would she live? Here in the sheriff's office with only a bed and no kitchen?

227

He put his head in his right hand while his left arm throbbed. Before he approached her about staying here, he'd have to find a decent deputy who would stay over nights for him. Then Josiah could have a place of his own and not have to sleep at the jail. Oh! Then he could buy Annie's ranch. It would be perfect! Maybe he could have Jenna after all. His mood lightened.

Josiah picked up his head and discovered he had a smile on his face. That was his first smile since discovering that Jenna was from another time. He had hope! And he felt happy.

Then Annie came through the door. He smiled at her and was about to tell her that he wanted to look at the ranch, when she spoke.

"Hallo, Sheriff. I have sold my ranch. I want to move into the 'teacher's house' as soon as possible."

Didn't the woman ever smile, wondered Josiah. "I'll get him out today, Annie. You can move into it tomorrow, but you'll probably have some clean up to do —Rawlins is a drunk, after all."

"I'll do what I have to do, Sheriff. Thank you." She turned to go back out the still open door.

"Annie," said Josiah, standing up in case he had to catch her, "who bought it?"

"Someone from away," said Annie and closed the door behind her.

Josiah's heart sank. Buying Annie's ranch would have made the whole plan so much easier. Now what? He wasn't willing to give up that easily. Now that he thought he had a chance with Jenna, he would move forward. Maybe he could buy some property and build his own place. That was a possibility. Meanwhile, he could look for a new deputy. He could ride out to the nearby towns and put the word out. There was always that fella, Nick, who helped him yesterday. But what were the chances he would want to come back to the nineteenth century to work?

And who was he, anyway? A friend of Jenna's? Josiah wondered how close a friend he was. And that gave him a funny feeling in his stomach. A bad feeling.

CHAPTER FIFTY-FOUR

JENNA WANTED EVERYTHING prepared for Eliza's visit Wednesday. First she stopped at both coin dealers to cash in two of her three gold coins. She didn't want to take all their old silver, in case they couldn't get any more by Wednesday. The larger coin shop assured her that she could cash at least two more gold coins—with silver coins—by Wednesday.

Then she listed places to go and things to do while Eliza was in her century. She didn't think they would get to all of them, but she'd give a brief overview to Eliza and let her decide. Although Jenna would have loved to take her to a movie theater, that would take a couple of hours that they could go other places instead. That was out, then.

She wondered about Eliza's "old clothes" while she was here. Jenna decided that she would wear an old-time dress, also. Everyone would think they were participating in an event with the Victorian Society.

Wednesday came before she felt ready for it. She wondered if it was a mistake agreeing to bring Eliza to her time—*her* Red Bluff. It didn't matter if it was a mistake or not. Jenna had promised to bring her, and today was the day.

Jenna arrived in the old Red Bluff at ten o'clock and left Magic in front of the school. She walked in and stood at the door until Annie acknowledged her. Annie excused herself from the class and met Jenna outside.

"I'm all moved out. You're welcome to move in after you pay me." When Jenna dug in her pocket, Annie stopped her. "No, not exactly pay me. I've arranged with Mr. Smythe at the bank to give you the deed of sale when you pay him the money. That way it's all legal and everything."

"That's fine, Annie. Can I ask you why you sold the ranch?"

"I want to leave town. I've always wanted to live in a bigger city, so this was my first step. I've already sent letters of application to several schools in different cities. I'd like to find someone to take over at school first. But if I can't, I've decided that I'll leave anyway.

"Is this transaction still a secret then?" Annie asked.

"Yes, Annie, I'd appreciate that."

"No problem. Good-bye," and without so much as a smile between them, Annie walked back into the class-room and closed the door behind her.

Jenna walked directly to the hotel and entered. Eliza was at the front desk.

"I'm ready! I'm ready!" said Eliza.

"My horse is down by the school. I have to go to the bank for a minute. Shall I meet you by the school?"

"Perfect," said Eliza. "I'll be there in a few minutes."

"Don't forget your gold coin!" said Jenna.

Eliza put her hand in her pocket and held up the gold coin. "That's the first thing I did this morning! See you soon. I can't wait!"

Jenna walked briskly up the street toward the bank. She hoped that Josiah was busy and wouldn't notice her. She asked for Mr. Smythe, and the man who came out surprised her.

He actually looked like a banker. A nineteenth-century banker, to be sure, but still a banker. Mr. Smythe wore a black suit with a striped shirt, spoke with a slight unknown accent, and was all business. He guided her into his sparse office that had a desk and a chair on each side of it.

Jenna sat down and counted out two thousand dollars in silver dollars, half dollars, and quarters. And Mr. Smythe not only recounted them, but examined every one. He even bit one between his teeth.

"What are you looking for, Mr. Smythe?" Jenna asked.

"Counterfeit," he said and kept on counting. Finally, he had all the coins stacked in hundred dollar stacks. When he finished, he said, "It's all here. Congratulations, Mrs. —?"

"Miss," Jenna said. "Miss Jenna Leyton."

Mr. Smythe cast a discriminating eye over Jenna and when he thought he approved of her, he handed her the deed of sale. "Look it over to make sure it looks all right."

Jenna didn't know what it should look like, but she thought it looked legitimate. "Looks fine to me," she said.

"Nice doing business with you, Miss Leyton. Good day to you." And with that, Mr. Smythe gathered papers on his desk and proceeded to ignore her. She smiled to herself, hugged the deed of sale to her chest, and walked out.

Eliza waited for her in front of the school. She was on

her horse already, an old chestnut mare. And the smile on her face was enough to light half the town of Red Bluff. It made Jenna smile even more.

"Let's go the back way, Eliza," said Jenna. "I don't want to run into Josiah accidentally."

They walked their horses back past the livery stable, down the block, across toward the main street, and out to the main road. Jenna took a quick look back to see if Josiah was walking down the street, but the street was empty. They passed the back of the Red Bluff sign and were soon on the side trail to the cave.

"I'm so excited!" said Eliza. "Is this the way to the cave?"

"Almost there," said Jenna. Then the cave appeared.

Jenna guided Magic in first, and Eliza followed. Jenna pointed out the fence panel that Hilary Clinton had used for the cattle.

"At what point in the cave does it change to your time?" asked Eliza. "I want to know the exact minute!"

"Josiah asked the same question. I have no idea." Jenna walked out through the other side of the cave. Eliza followed. "We're in my time, now, Eliza."

Eliza clapped her hands. "Where are the trucks?"

Jenna laughed. "You'll have to wait awhile for that. I was going to take you for a ride in the car, though. Would you like that?"

"I can't wait!" said Eliza.

CHAPTER FIFTY-FIVE

Jenna brought Eliza into the house and amazed her with all the differences in a twenty-first-century home. She showed her the refrigerator, the flat-top electric stove, and the dishwasher. Then she demonstrated the microwave for her and wowed her with the central heating and the television. Eliza especially liked cartoons. But when Jenna showed her the bathroom, Eliza couldn't get over it. She wanted to keep flushing the toilet to watch the water swirl around and go down. And when the toilet paper delighted her, Jenna gave her a couple of rolls to take back with her.

Next, they got into the car, and Jenna drove to the coin dealer's. Although Eliza held on to the dashboard the whole way, she enjoyed the ride. At the coin dealer's, Eliza exchanged her one gold coin for fifteen hundred dollars worth of old silver coins, all minted before 1870. Except one. Eliza chose one coin minted in 1912 for a keepsake. It made Jenna laugh.

Jenna then took her to lunch at a restaurant with a huge menu. It took Eliza ten minutes to decide what to eat. And the separate dessert menu took her another ten minutes to decide. Finally, they arrived back at Jenna's house to find Granny's car in the driveway.

When they walked into the house, Jenna called out, "Granny?"

Granny walked out of the kitchen with a cup of hot tea in her hand and said, "I'm right here, Jenna. No need to wake the dead!" Then she saw Eliza. "Oh, excuse me. I didn't know Jenna had company."

"Granny, this is Eliza, from the nineteenth century. Eliza, this is my grandmother."

"Nice to meet you, Eliza. I've heard that you're taking good care of my granddaughter over there. She can be a handful sometimes, can't she? Would you like a cup of tea, Eliza?"

"Will you make it in the wavy thing?" asked Eliza.

"Microwave," said Jenna.

"No, I make it the old fashioned way by heating water on the stove, but we can use the microwave, if you want."

After making tea, the three women sat at the kitchen table, sipping tea and talking. Eliza talked about all the wonders she had seen since she arrived.

When the conversation slowed down, Granny asked, "Jenna, what about that man of yours?"

"He got shot—not hurt bad—just a flesh wound. Kat was there to help the doctor, so it worked out fine. But he still doesn't want me around. Even making him jealous didn't work."

"Maybe," said Granny, "you need to take the next step. Ignore him completely! He asked you to leave him alone, then leave him alone. Don't look at him, don't talk to him. But be sure to talk to everyone else around him so he sees it. If that doesn't work, you might as well

235

forget him! He's hopeless!"

"I agree, Jenna. That's a good idea. And if it doesn't work, I'll find someone else for you! Josiah would be perfect, but if he's too stubborn to come around, then you have to move on." Eliza hesitated and then said, "Granny, what is your first name? I don't know what to call you."

"Just call me Granny. Everybody does. Except the people who swear at me, and I won't tell you what *they* call me!"

"Okay, Granny! We have enjoyed Jenna so much. She comes every weekend and has supper with us. Oh, will you be coming Friday, Jenna?"

"No, I can't. Saturday is Granny's birthday."

"You don't have to miss out on your friends and your fun for me, Jenna. I stopped officially having birthdays when I was twenty-nine, anyway!"

"Jenna," Eliza spoke slowly like she was still focusing her thoughts, "why don't we have a birthday party for Granny at the hotel? It would be fun!"

"A birthday bash honoring me? I like the sound of that!" said Granny.

"Oh, Granny, you can't go. The only way to get there is on horseback."

"Jenna! Didn't we go through this before? I taught you to ride a horse! I bet I could still beat you at those barrels out there!"

"Okay, okay, you can ride. How can we arrange it?"

"Samuel and I will do all the arranging and cook all the food. You invite everyone you want, and we'll invite everyone in town. It will be loads of fun!"

"Oh, Eliza. That would be too expensive. I can't ask you to do that."

236

Eliza jingled the coins in her pocket. "Not too expensive at all, Jenna! And with these," she jingled the coins again, "I can even hire someone to help. It will be a great party!"

"For a great person," said Granny. "Me!"

"My dad will love you!" said Eliza.

"I know," said Jenna. "They're two of a kind."

"Okay," Granny said, standing up, "you two work out the details. I have to get home now. Very nice meeting you, Eliza. And I will look forward to seeing you Saturday!"

Eliza stood up and hugged Granny. "Nice meeting you, too, Granny. And I'm looking forward to your party!"

Granny walked out of the room and left the two women at the table. Eliza sighed. "What a wonderful day this has been. And I'm so looking forward to your grandmother's party! I haven't done a party in so long." She sighed again. "It's been way too long."

Eliza stood up, placed her cup in the sink, and said, "Will you take me back now, Jenna? It's been a full day, and I'm tired."

"Sure, Eliza. Would you like to use the bathroom first?"

Eliza clapped her hands. "Oh yeah! That was fun!" She turned around and looked at the different doors. "Where is it? I'm confused."

Jenna led her into the bathroom off the living room. "You can use this one."

Eliza poked her head in and stepped back out. "You have two bathrooms in one house? I love it!" She walked in and closed the door behind her.

Back on the trail, the two women talked and planned

237

the party, and then rode awhile in silence. Then Eliza spoke.

"Jenna, dear, I have to say something that's on my heart."

"Go ahead, Eliza, I'm listening."

"Now that I've been to your world, I don't think it would work out between you and Josiah."

That took Jenna aback. "Why not?" she said almost indignantly.

"Jenna, you know how fond I am of you. But this world of yours," she waved her hands around, "how could you leave it? How could you give up a warm bathroom with soap for a drafty outhouse? How could you give up your wavy thing for a smoky wood cooking stove? How could you live in our world after living in yours? And you couldn't expect Josiah to live here. He wouldn't fit in here at all."

"I can fit in, Eliza, because it's what I've always wanted—to live back in the cowboy times. I know there are some inconveniences, but I don't care. I just bought that ranch, didn't I? I've already decided. Whether anything happens with Josiah or not, I'm moving into your century. It will be difficult seeing him around, but it's what I want. I want to live there."

"What about your grandmother? You'll miss her."

"I can come back to visit whenever I want. And once she rides over there, she may want to visit me sometimes. We'll see each other often enough."

"You sound determined, Jenna. Okay then! If it doesn't work out with Josiah, we'll find you another man!"

They had emerged from the cave and were walking on the main road. When they came to the Red Bluff sign,

Eliza said, "Thank you, Jenna, for a wonderful day. And thanks for the money!" She jingled the coins in her pocket. "I feel like a thief with all this extra cash! You can return now; I can find my way from here. And I'll see you Saturday! Bye!" Eliza leaned over and hugged Jenna.

"We'll bring the dessert, Eliza!"

"But I'll make the birthday cake, Jenna!" Eliza called back as she rode down the trail.

CHAPTER FIFTY-SIX

JOSIAH FELT ELATED. Now that he had decided that maybe it could work with Jenna, he was busy preparing for having her in his life. He'd already ridden out to the nearest two towns and asked the sheriff of each if he knew anyone who might want to be deputy—and wasn't a drinker. He didn't want to have to deal with another Rawlins situation. Although he could have sent them a telegram, he thought it would be better if he asked in person.

Thinking of Rawlins, he hated that he was around him all the time now. Or at least around him whenever he wasn't at the saloon drinking. Since the poor drunk had nowhere else to go, Josiah offered to let him sleep in a jail cell. And Rawlins had accepted. So now he was back there snoring away and bothering Josiah. Although he was in the farthest cell from the door, Josiah could still hear the snoring, even with the door closed. When Josiah found a new deputy, he didn't know what he'd do with Rawlins. But he didn't have to worry about that yet.

The next step for Josiah was to look for property that he could buy and find someone to help him build a house. If he could take some time off, he could build it himself. Unfortunately, that wasn't possible right now. Even if he found a new deputy, it would take time to break him in right.

After spending two days riding around trying to find some land that would suit him and Jenna, he still hadn't found anything close. And he had been out riding so much that he hadn't had supper with Eliza and Samuel all week. And still he hadn't found anything. If he was too far from town, it would defeat the purpose anyway. He wanted someplace close enough that he could ride to after a day's work and for Jenna to ride to town easily.

Annie's place would have been perfect for him and Jenna. He felt so disappointed in himself for not moving on that sooner. But he found it strange that Annie would not tell who bought her ranch. She was never talkative, but keeping secrets like this seemed out of the ordinary. And why would anyone want to keep that secret? The whole notion puzzled Josiah.

He had taken a ride out to the ranch after Annie moved into the school housing, but no one was there. The barn was empty, but he could see all the furniture still inside the house. Whoever bought it must have bought the furniture with it. Maybe someone from back east bought it. Then everything would make more sense. Maybe someone was moving in and planning to start a new business in town. That had to be the answer, and that would be great. His little town was growing.

Frustrated with the situation, but happy about his decision to go forward with Jenna, he thought he wasn't going to ask her to marry him yet. He wanted to get more in place before that. But maybe he could get her up on the roof again for another kiss. Josiah smiled at the thought.

And she'd be here tomorrow afternoon. It seemed funny. Less than a week ago he begged her not to come back and not to see him again. And now he couldn't wait to see her. His smile faded. What if she had decided to listen to him and not return here? No, Jenna was too much of a rebel for that. She had even kissed him again the last time that he saw her. What if it was a good-bye kiss? Now he felt scared. It would serve him right if she didn't come back after the way he treated her. But he ached for her, wanted her so bad that he couldn't stand it.

Abruptly, Josiah stood and stomped out the door. It slammed behind him, and he didn't care if he woke Rawlins or not. He had to get to the hotel.

Stepping through the door of the hotel, he looked around for Eliza. Not seeing her, he knocked on the door frame leading to her sitting room. Then he called out.

"Eliza! Eliza!"

Eliza rushed into the room holding her floured hands up. "Yes, Josiah. What is it? I'm busy in the back preparing for a birthday party."

"Oh, well, I wanted to ask if Jenna was coming to supper tomorrow night."

"No, she isn't. Now I have to run. I have a lot to do." She returned to the kitchen.

Josiah followed. "Why isn't she coming, Eliza? Because of what I said to her?"

"I wouldn't blame her if she didn't come back after the way you acted, Josiah Stone! But, no, that's not it." She went back to working in the flour.

"Well, why then? Why isn't Jenna coming tomorrow night?" said Josiah, exasperated.

"Because she's preparing for her grandmother's birthday Saturday, and so am I. Oh, by the way, you're invited. It starts at eleven."

"Jenna's *grandmother* is coming here?"

"Don't act so surprised, Josiah. It's not that long a trip."

"What! How do you know it's not that long a trip?" Josiah asked.

Eliza winked at him. "Wouldn't you like to know?" she chided him.

Josiah ignored her comment. She couldn't possibly have gone to Jenna's time. It didn't make any sense. Why would Jenna do that?

"Do you know if that fellow, Nick, is coming to the party?"

"I imagine so. She's bringing a bunch of people, and I've invited almost the whole town. It should be fun."

"Okay, thanks, Eliza," said Josiah.

CHAPTER FIFTY-SEVEN

JENNA WASN'T SURE she could finish everything in time for Saturday, but she did. First she had to call everyone to make sure they could attend the party. Then she had to buy all the desserts that she planned to bring, and also buy several more soft-sided coolers to carry the desserts. She bought three half-gallons of Rocky Road, one plastic gallon container of chocolate and one of vanilla, a half-gallon of strawberry, a half-gallon of neapolitan, and a half-gallon of chocolate mint. Then she bought three of the checkerboard cakes, one chocolate and one vanilla cake, and several pies including lemon meringue and chocolate cream.

Although it was last minute, everyone she called said they could attend, including Rachel. Her friend, Rachel, and Kat's daughter, Madison, were the only ones besides Granny who hadn't yet visited the nineteenth century.

Jenna had invited Rachel because she was an out-of-work schoolteacher, presently working as a substitute when she could. Jenna thought that if Annie was leaving, Rachel might want a full-time job badly enough to be willing to live in the nineteenth century. Jenna didn't mention the teaching job to her because Annie hadn't left yet. There was no reason to get Rachel's hopes up. For now, she just wanted Rachel to get the feel of the old Red Bluff.

Now that everything was in place—the horses saddled and the coolers packed—Jenna waited for everyone to arrive. Nick arrived first, and Jenna was grateful for that. He brought two of his horses because with so many people, all the horses in Jenna's barn were already spoken for. Nick unloaded his striking pinto and the bay, both already saddled and ready to go. Then Kat and Madison arrived, then Rachel, and then Ryan.

But where was the guest of honor? Jenna ran back into the house to call Granny. The phone rang and rang, and no one answered. Then Jenna saw out the window that Granny had arrived. She wore a long dress reminiscent of the nineteenth century. Kat, Madison, and Rachel all had long dresses on. Kat and Rachel were in the Victorian Society with her, and Madison could have borrowed one of Kat's long dresses. But Granny dressing like that was a surprise.

"Beautiful dress, Granny! Where'd you get it?"

"A friend of mine bought it for me on eBay, if you have to know!" Granny said with annoyance.

Jenna and everyone else laughed.

"What's wrong with you people? You don't know what eBay is? Or you don't think that I do? I was shopping at eBay before all of you were born!"

"Oh, Granny, eBay isn't that old. But happy birthday!"

Everyone else chimed in and said, "Happy Birthday" to Granny, too.

"Oh stop that! I told you that I stopped officially having birthdays when I was twenty-nine."

"Then Granny, why did you agree to this *birthday* party?"

"Because I figured it was the only way to get Jenna to let me go back to the nineteenth century, and I've been dying to go! Now let's saddle up and get going before you make me miss my own damn party!"

Everyone mounted their horses, still giggling over Granny's outburst. But they all knew her well enough to know there was nothing behind it. She was soft as a pillow on the inside.

They rode down the trail, all the horses laden with a cooler, except Dolly, the horse that Granny rode. Jenna wasn't taking any chances. Granny insisted on leading the way with Jenna, even though Dolly had a slow gait. Jenna supposed that it was because Granny was used to being first at almost everything she did. Especially riding a horse.

The group went through the cave, and Jenna announced they were almost there. Then when the Red Bluff sign came up, Granny got really excited.

"I can't believe we're here. In the nineteenth century! It's what I've always wanted," she said dreamily.

"You mean to visit the old Red Bluff?"

"No, I mean to live in the old times like this," said Granny.

"You never told me that before," said Jenna.

"What's to tell? I don't go around talking about something that can't happen. I hear enough complaining from the old fogies that I hang around with. I'm not going to add to the complaints of this world!"

Jenna smiled. Her Granny was an original, but Eliza's father, Edward, was a close second. He and Granny were like two peas in a pod.

"Since we're going to be here all afternoon, should we drop the horses off at the livery stable?" asked Jenna.

"We need to unload all the coolers, Jen," said Ryan. "How about if we stop in front of the hotel, unload, and then Nick and I will take the horses to the livery?"

"Sounds good, Ryan, thanks." Jenna got off Magic and then helped Granny off Dolly.

Granny pulled away. "I can do it myself, girl!" Then she nearly stumbled taking her other foot out of the stirrup. Jenna caught her, but didn't say a word.

When Jenna and the other women approached the hotel door, they saw a big sign that said, "Restaurant Closed! Party! But YOU'RE invited! Come on in!"

CHAPTER FIFTY-EIGHT

JOSIAH, STANDING ACROSS the room talking to Edward, saw Jenna come in the door and felt a warmth spread through his body. He loved her so much. How did he ever consider living without her? It would be impossible, he knew that now. Edward was in the middle of a story that Josiah had already heard several times, but Josiah thought it would be polite to keep listening. Even from here, he could watch her and enjoy her presence.

Josiah watched as Jenna hugged Eliza and introduced her to the four people with her. He only recognized Kat, who he thought was Jenna's sister. Nick and the other man, who he had seen her with before, were nowhere around. Glancing out the window, he saw them leading several horses down the street. Oh good, he thought, he could talk to Nick about becoming a deputy.

As Edward rambled on, Josiah tried to edge him across the room. For a few minutes it worked, and then Edward stood his ground and said, "Why are you push-ing me across the dang room?" Edward turned his head and saw the group of women surrounding Eliza. "Oh, your woman is here now. Who's that old bag with her? Is that her grandmother?"

"I imagine so. Wouldn't you like to go over there and meet her?" asked Josiah.

"It would probably be polite since it's her birthday," said Edward.

They walked across the room toward the group of women. Josiah noticed that when Jenna raised her head from talking and saw him, she turned away without acknowledging him. Kat and the two other women followed Jenna as she walked away, but Jenna's grandmother continued talking to Eliza.

When they reached them, Eliza introduced Josiah and Edward to Granny, who took one look at Josiah and said, "So you're the handsome but stubborn little snot who's rebuffing my granddaughter. You better be careful, dude, or you're going to lose her!" Then she turned her attention to Edward.

"And I am the one you've been waiting for all your life, sweet lady," said Edward as he kissed her hand and bowed.

"Now why would I be waiting for an old fart like you?" asked Granny. Edward had some witty response for Granny, but Josiah was already walking away trying to follow Jenna.

He saw her look back over her shoulder at him and keep walking. Then the front door opened, and Nick and Ryan walked in.

"Hallo, Nick. Good to see you again."

"Sheriff, this is my friend, Ryan. He's Jenna's brother."

"Hi, Ryan. Nice meeting you. Nick, I wanted to thank you for coming to my aid the other day."

"No problem, Sheriff, it's what I do—you know—back on the other side. It looks like you're all patched up. Does

249

it hurt much?" asked Nick.

"Not much any more. I heal quick. Nick, I wanted to ask you if you'd be interested in a job as a deputy? I know you live *over there*, but I thought maybe occasionally or on weekends or something. What do you think?"

"I'm going to let you two discuss the possibilities," said Ryan as he walked away and joined the party. Josiah saw him head straight across the room toward Mary Elizabeth.

"I've always wanted to be a cowboy!" said Nick. "I will give it some thought. It sounds like fun. The shooting incident that happened the other day—how often does that happen around here?"

"Not often, anymore. It happened almost every day when I first came to town. A lot has changed since then."

"Would I have to handle it the same way you did? I'm not fond of standing in front of two men with guns."

"Nick, you can handle it however you like, as long as you stop it. I don't want *any* of that going on in my town."

"Understood. Well, let me think about it, and I'll get back to you," said Nick. "Right now, I want to join the party! See ya!"

Josiah smiled as Nick walked away. He was happy that Nick would consider being a part-time deputy. That was a start. At least he didn't discount the whole idea. Now he wanted to find Jenna and talk to her.

She had managed to get clear across the room again. As he made his way over there, he realized that he didn't know what he was going to say to her. But he decided that he would just let his heart speak. He hoped it didn't reveal too much.

When he finally reached her, she said a curt hallo and

then introduced him to her friend, Rachel, and to Madison, Kat's daughter. When he edged closer to her, Kat asked him something and Madison wanted to look at his badge. Jenna got away.

Fifteen minutes later, he was grateful when Sarah walked over and started talking to the three women. He tipped his hat and walked away, looking for Jenna as he walked. Again she was across the room from him, talking to Ryan and Mary Elizabeth.

He approached and felt as if he was intruding. So he stepped next to Jenna and said, "Jenna, can I talk to you for a minute?"

"Maybe later, Josiah, right now I have to go talk to Henry and Annie. Bye."

Jenna walked a few paces away and started talking to Henry and Annie. Henry and Annie? Why would Jenna have to talk to them? She didn't even like Henry! Was she deliberately avoiding him? He'd wait awhile longer and try again.

He walked away and saw Samuel standing by a table loaded with desserts. Samuel was eating more of the checkerboard cake and that ice cream with the marshmallows and nuts in it. Josiah thought he might as well eat some while he waited for Jenna.

As he stood there, Matthew, the saloon owner, and Sarah walked up to him. Matthew had a plate of something yellow and white.

"Josiah! You have to try this pie! It's wonderful!" said Matthew.

"It's called lemon meringue pie, Josiah. I'll get you some," said Sarah, and she walked away to the next table.

"Who's watching the saloon, Matthew?" asked Josiah.

251

"Young Zack. I told him I'd relieve him after a while. But I'm enjoying myself and especially enjoying these wonderful desserts! I'm not leaving yet!"

Sarah reappeared with a plate of the yellow and white pie and another piece of chocolate looking pie squished next to it.

"You will *love* this, Josiah! Trust me on this! Here." She handed him the plate and a fork.

Josiah took one bite of each piece of pie and couldn't stop eating. Each of them was different but delicious, and possibly even better than the cake and ice cream. When he finished eating the two pieces of pie a minute later, he put the empty plate on the table and exhaled. He felt stuffed, and he hadn't had any regular food at all. Well, how often did he get such delicious desserts as these?

As he was about to walk away, Kat and her daughter, Madison, walked up and started talking to Sarah. Matthew stepped closer to Josiah, and they talked between themselves for a few minutes. Then Sarah came over and asked Matthew to step away for a minute.

Sarah walked back to Kat and Madison and said that Matthew wanted to ask Madison something. Matthew came over then and said, "Madison, would you mind going across the street to the saloon and telling Zack, the young man there, to lock up the cash register, and come on over here? I'd appreciate it if you could do that."

Madison was grateful to get away and hurried from the room and out the door. Josiah looked at everyone and raised his eyebrows.

"I'm doing some matchmaking," said Sarah. "I think they will like each other."

"Madison is involved with school right now, Sarah.

She's consumed with her studies. *Boys* are the farthest thing from her mind," said Kat.

"You never know!" said Sarah.

Josiah spotted Jenna across the room speaking to Eliza and Granny. He walked up to them and was about to speak when Eliza said, "Josiah, we have to sing Granny a birthday song. Can you get everyone's attention? Wait until we get over by the cake. Eliza, Jenna, and Granny walked over to the table where a large birthday cake sat with a large container of chocolate ice cream next to it. Eliza lit thirteen candles, seven on the top and six on the bottom, for seventy-six. The extra one was for good luck. Eliza nodded her head to Josiah.

He clapped his hands and tried to get the large crowd to quiet down. He tried yelling, and that didn't work either. No one could hear him over the din. But Nick, who was standing close by, heard him. He put two fingers in his mouth and whistled a shrill sound that caught everyone's attention. Josiah definitely liked that guy.

"Okay, everybody, it's time to sing the birthday song to Granny. Is everybody ready?"

"Years ago on this very day
A babe was born, hurray hurray.
Now it's time to celebrate
what happened on this very date.
And honor one who's here today
And all of us are here to say,
Happy Birthday, Granny!"

The crowd screamed, and a few men threw their hats in the air. Granny blew out the candles, but Edward surprised her when he came up from behind, turned her

253

around, and kissed her on the mouth.

"You cad," she said and slapped him. Then she grabbed him by his shirt and pulled him close to her. "Kiss me again!" So he did. Everyone in the room broke out into mad laughter.

CHAPTER FIFTY-NINE

JOSIAH HAD BEEN following her around all evening. Jenna had done her best to avoid him but was running out of excuses. And she realized that it was more than just Granny's advice to ignore him and talk to everyone else. She felt angry with him. Josiah talking to her in that tone of voice, telling her repeatedly to leave him alone and not return to Red Bluff. And now, suddenly, he was following her around like a little puppy. Well, she wouldn't have any part of it. She would tell Eliza that she wouldn't be coming the next weekend.

Jenna looked around the room. Everybody was having a great time. Everyone loved the desserts, and the people from the new Red Bluff were talking to the people from the old Red Bluff. What a great idea of Eliza's to have this party. Where was Granny, anyway? Glancing around the room, she noticed that several people were missing, including Granny, Ryan, Henry, and Rachel. Wait, there was Rachel talking to Annie. Oh, good. That might work out for both of them, whenever Annie gets around to leaving.

Josiah came up unexpectedly behind her. Putting his

hand on her shoulder, he turned her around to face him.

"Jenna, we need to talk."

Jenna pulled away from his grasp and said, "I don't need anything, Josiah, except to eat something." Then she walked to the food table without giving him the satisfaction of seeing her looking back.

The food table held several varieties of meats, some vegetables, and biscuits that were no longer warm. Sarah came over to join her.

"What a great party! Granny must be loving all the attention," said Sarah.

"I don't know where she wandered off to. But last I saw her, she was having a blast! Hey, Sarah, without being too obvious can you look around and see where Josiah is? He was right behind me."

Deliberately looking in the opposite direction first, Sarah scanned the crowd. In a slightly elevated voice, she said, "I don't see Granny, either." Then, making her voice quieter, she said, "He's twenty feet away looking this way. He looks like someone's stolen his new kitten. What happened?"

"He's followed me around all night wanting to talk. Last week he told me he never wanted to see me again. I'm just angry. Just because he's ready to talk now doesn't mean that I have to bend to his wishes. He's not calling the shots, here."

"That's my friend, Jenna!" Sarah said, patting Jenna on the shoulder. "Rebel to the end!"

"It's getting late. Let's circle the room to get away from sheriff-boy over there and get closer to the door of the restaurant. Maybe I can slip out without him noticing."

Toward the other side of the room, just past the

dessert tables, Rachel was talking to Annie. When Jenna and Sarah approached them, Rachel gave them a big grin.

"I'm back to work!" said Rachel.

"I wondered if that would interest you, Rachel. Annie is thinking of leaving," said Jenna.

"I *am* leaving!" said Annie with the first smile Jenna had ever seen on her face. "I'm getting married, and we're moving to the city!"

"Who are you marrying?" asked Jenna.

Annie looked toward the door and said, "Henry. I've always liked him—he was so friendly and nice—but I thought with a store that he'd be wanting to stay in town here. But he's sold his store, so we're leaving Red Bluff!"

"Who's buying his store?" asked Sarah.

Henry and Ryan walked up to the three women. "He is," said Henry with his hand on Ryan's back.

"Ryan! What about *your* store?" asked Jenna.

"Sold," said Ryan. "It's final in two weeks, but they're taking over sooner, which is fine with me. That way I can work on, um, some stuff for you, Jenna."

Jenna was grateful that he hadn't slipped about her new ranch. "But a general store! Why a general store?"

"Because there are fewer people here, and I should have more time to paint. Which reminds me, where's Edward? I brought some new oil paints for him."

"I don't know, but Granny's missing, too," said Jenna. "Well, congratulations on your marriage, Henry and Annie."

Henry put his arm around Annie and hugged her to him. "Don't you just love her? I've had my eye on her for years, but assumed she wanted to stay at her ranch in Red Bluff. When I found out she had sold the ranch, I made my move! Now she's going to be my wife! I couldn't be more thrilled."

Jenna didn't want him to go on and on again, so she figured she should make her exit before he started talking about something else. "Well, good luck to you both. Rachel, Ryan, we'll be leaving soon. And congratulations to you, too, Ryan, on your new business!"

Jenna walked away, and Sarah followed. So far she had managed to evade Josiah. They reached the door, and Jenna looked around the room for Eliza.

"Ah oh," said Sarah. "Look who's coming down the stairs."

Jenna looked. It was Granny and Edward. "I wonder what they were doing up there," said Jenna.

"I don't know, but they're both glowing!" said Sarah.

"Oh, you don't suppose—"

"There you are!" said Eliza. "I've been looking for you all afternoon. Are you enjoying the party? More important, is Granny enjoying the party?"

Jenna moved away from the doorway so Eliza could look out. Granny and Edward were almost to the bottom of the stairs.

"You tell me, Eliza!" said Jenna.

Eliza put her hand to her mouth and giggled. Then they all laughed.

Jenna saw Josiah a few feet away approaching them. Ah, this is perfect, she thought.

"Eliza, I wanted to thank you for the party and tell you that I won't be coming to visit next weekend. I have some chores to do—at home," said Jenna.

"Child, don't make me come get you! We miss you when you're not here. Please come again soon," said Eliza.

"Sometime," said Jenna vaguely.

"Jenna, can we talk before you leave? Please?" said Josiah as he stepped up to the women.

"I'm sorry, Josiah, maybe another time. I need to take my grandmother home. We need to return before dark." Turning to Granny, who was now in the doorway, she said, "Are you ready to leave, Granny?"

"Not really," she said as she smiled up at Edward, "but I suppose if I say no, you'll drag my butt out of here."

"Where's Kat?" asked Jenna.

"Last time I saw her, she was in a heated conversation with Doc Mercer," said Eliza.

"Here comes almost everybody, Jenna. Ryan is bringing Kat and Rachel," said Sarah.

"There's Nick saying good-bye to our good sheriff," said Eliza. "I don't know where Madison ran off to, though."

Kat, Rachel, and Ryan walked up to them. "We need to stop at the saloon and pick up Madison," said Kat.

Nick joined them, and Josiah stared at Jenna with a gloomy expression on his face. "Everybody ready?" asked Nick. "Ryan and I can get the horses and meet you back here."

"We can all walk," said Jenna. "Work off some of that dessert! Oh, Granny, do you want to wait here?"

"What, you think my legs have fallen off because I turned seventy-five? I can walk like everybody else!"

"I'll walk with you, Bea," said Edward.

"Of course you will! I wouldn't expect anything less!"

"Ryan, thank you for the paints! I'm eager to start working in oils again!"

"Now that I'll have the store here in town, you'll never be without oils again!" said Ryan.

They all walked out the front door of the hotel and strolled down the street. Kat ducked into the saloon to call Madison. Jenna gave a quick glance behind her and saw that Granny and Edward were holding hands and laughing as they walked. That made Jenna smile. This was a great day for Granny, and Jenna was grateful that Eliza had suggested it. She'd have to bring Granny back here again soon.

Ezra brought all the horses out, and everyone mounted up except Granny. She stood to the side with Edward, both of them looking into each other's eyes and talking softly.

Edward helped Granny mount Dolly and then smiled at her. As all the horses started walking down the street, Edward yelled out, "When are you coming back here, you ole hag?"

"Not soon enough for my taste, you ole fart!" answered Granny.

Jenna heard Granny giggle as they rode away down the road, back to another time and another life.

CHAPTER SIXTY

BACK AT HOME, after relaxing the day after Granny's party, Jenna felt restless. She wasn't sure she had done the right thing with Josiah. Maybe she should have listened to what he had to say. But if he just wanted to tell her again not to return to *his* Red Bluff, it would kill her. She couldn't take that. Especially after she'd bought the property. And she was looking forward to living there. It would be an adventure. A better adventure after Ryan had put in the composting toilet, though.

If she was going to move into that house with the intention of living there, she'd have to move some of her belongings over there. And moving meant packing. She had some small soft-sided luggage that she could use. It would take a few trips to move everything, though. Of course, what was her hurry? There were no closets there, except the one chifforobe. Did it even have hangers in it? Did they hang up clothes back then, or put them on pegs? Well, it didn't matter. Hangers or pegs, there wasn't room for many, so she'd bring fewer clothes. That didn't strike her as a big deal. It would kill Sarah, thought Jenna. Sarah never wore the same outfit twice!

After she had all her clothes spread out on the bed in the spare room, she wondered what else around the house she needed to bring. None of the electronic devices could go. She'd miss her laptop and her iPod. She'd need cooking utensils. It didn't matter to her whether Annie left hers or not. There were some items that Jenna *must* have. Although she didn't know if you could cook in a wood stove with glass cookware, she decided that heat was heat, so she lined up all her casserole dishes at the side of the bed. Jenna thought she'd bring a couple of mugs this trip and bring more next trip if Annie hadn't left any dishes. Then she decided to buy some paper plates. She didn't want to bother with moving fragile dishes if she didn't have to. Shoes! She'd need more shoes than just her cowboy boots, although that's what she wore most of the time.

That should be it for the first trip. She'd wrap the fragile items into the clothing to keep them safe and only take one suitcase this time. She would only stay long enough to put these items away and visit with Eliza. If she stayed overnight, she'd stay at the hotel. Maybe Eliza would have some insight about Josiah. Jenna didn't feel optimistic right now. And that made her sad.

Her phone rang. When she picked it up, Kat was on the line. She sounded excited.

"Jenna! I thought of the greatest idea for you! Even better than a composting toilet!"

"Kat, you're so funny. Speaking as my nineteenth-century self, what could possibly be better than a composting toilet?"

"Solar energy!"

"I can't have those big honkin' things on my property. It would mess up the time continuum or something."

"Not the big ones, Jenna. They have small ones now that you can stick in a drawer when you don't want anyone to see them. They'd be perfect to give you some electricity. Google it! Have to run. Later! Love you. Bye."

And just like that Kat was off the line. Miniature solar power. Maybe she could keep her laptop and her iPod after all! And she could at least get a solar battery charger. She hadn't thought of that, but it would be perfect for some little items that she'd love to bring.

"Thank you, Kat!" Jenna said aloud.

The front door opened. "Where's Kat?" asked Granny. She carried a medium size soft-sided suitcase.

"She was on the phone, Granny, but she just gave me a great idea. Where are you going with that suitcase? Do you need a ride to the airport or something? Did I forget about a trip you had planned?"

"None of the above, Jenna, but I'd like you to saddle Dolly for me," said Granny.

"Hmmm, saddle Dolly. What's this about, Granny?"

"Jenna, if I've learned anything at my age, it is to seize the day. If something is bad, you stop doing it. If something is good, you do it as much as you can. I like Edward. He likes me. We have both lost our own true loves and are alone. We are both rapscallions. We belong together. We've talked about it, and we're getting married."

"Married? Granny, you just met him!" said Jenna.

"Time's a wastin', Jenna. At seventy-five, I know what I know, and so does he. We've decided, and I'm not letting you or anyone else talk me out of it. And neither is he. He's already arranged for a minister to marry us this weekend. You're welcome to come to our wedding, if you want. Now, will you saddle Dolly for me? I don't need her permanently. You can bring her back with you next time you visit."

"Wow, Granny," said Jenna taking a deep breath. "Give me a minute to take this all in. Okay, I'll go saddle Dolly. Is there anything else you want to take with you that I can help you with or bring later? Or do you want me to ride over there with you so you don't get lost?"

"I don't need a lot, and Edward's room is small. If we decide to move someplace bigger, I'll figure it out then. And as far as getting lost, I think I can find my way on these trails that *I blazed* before you were born! Thank you for asking."

Jenna walked out the door shaking her head. Well, at least she didn't have to miss Granny while she was in the nineteenth century. She'd be right there! As she brushed Dolly, she marveled at how everything was turning out. She had accidentally found the cave, had fallen in love with a cowboy in the nineteenth century, and had bought a ranch there; her brother had bought a store there, and her grandmother had fallen in love there—it was almost like it was all meant to be. Even Rachel, one of her good friends, was probably going to move there. Life could be strange.

When she finished brushing and saddling Dolly, she found Granny waiting behind her with her suitcase. "I would have brought that out for you, Granny, I'm sorry."

"I'm perfectly capable of carrying it on my own. I ain't dead yet!" and then she cackled with laughter. "Come on, hug me, Jenna. But don't get all teary-eyed, because I know I will see you soon."

Jenna hugged her and couldn't stop hugging. She knew she'd see her soon, but her grandmother moving to the nineteenth century felt momentous to her. She boost-

264

ed Granny up into the saddle, tied the suitcase on, and stepped back.

"Good-bye, Granny. I love you."

"Don't act like it's forever, Jenna. It's just a few days. And I have something to say about that handsome sheriff of yours. He'll come get you. He's no fool, that one. I saw it in his eyes. He's a good man, and I approve. You listen to me, girl. You two will be together before you know it. Maybe we'll even have a double wedding!" That made Granny cackle again. She turned Dolly around and waved good-bye.

Jenna walked into the house and started crying. She didn't even know why. But Granny's leaving had completely set her off. Granny's intuition was usually correct, so if she said that she and Josiah would be together, then there was a good chance they would be. Then why was she crying? And why couldn't she stop?

CHAPTER SIXTY-ONE

JOSIAH TIRED OF shuffling papers back and forth across his desk, so he paced from one side of the room to the other. Had he lost her forever? If they truly loved each other, couldn't they get past his mistake? He didn't understand it. If he was so in love with her why had he tried to push her away? Yes, he did understand. Who was he kidding? He was afraid. Especially afraid that someone from another time could easily leave him. Would he rather have someone who would stay with him because they had to? Or Jenna, who would stay because she wanted to. Or not.

He thought of the way she kept walking away from him at the party. Every time he approached, she would escape somehow. And he had driven her to that. He knew that, and now he would pay for it. Jenna said she wasn't coming back this weekend. What if she never came back? What would he do then? He couldn't live without her. Of that he was certain. If there was one woman for each man, then she was his. He'd never felt this way before and knew that he never would again.

There was only one choice. He had to go to her. As

much as he loved this Red Bluff, his Red Bluff, he realized it would be too lonely without her. Lonely enough that he was willing to leave his entire life behind and go live in her century. What would he do there? He had no idea, but it didn't matter. Being with Jenna was all that mattered. Everything else was secondary.

Josiah realized that he hadn't been breathing, so he exhaled slowly and drew in another deep breath. Now that he had decided to live in her time to be with her, he felt better. It wasn't an easy choice, but it was an obvious one. He couldn't do without her. And he didn't want to.

But how would he go to her? Just ride to the place where they had caught Hilary Clinton and ride around until he found her? No, he had no idea what awaited him in that world. That wouldn't work. And he needed to find her. It had to be soon—it had to be now.

He would talk to Eliza about it. Maybe she had more information than he did. He hoped so. Wait a minute. What was it that Eliza had said to Jenna? "Don't make me come get you." And she also said, "It's not that long a trip." Eliza had been there! That had to be what she meant! Eliza could help him!

Josiah walked out the door and down the street so fast that he forgot to close the door to his office. Walking back, he closed it gently. He felt so good, so happy, that he'd even let Rawlins sleep. Finally, he felt something that he hadn't felt in a while: hope.

Entering the hotel, he saw Eliza at the front desk. His smile spread across his whole face.

"Well, what's got into you, Josiah Stone? I would guess Jenna's ice cream and cake, but Samuel and I finished it last night."

"Please tell me where Jenna is," said Josiah. "I need to

go to her—right away."

"What makes you think I know where Jenna is?" asked Eliza.

"Because you said to her, 'Don't make me come get you.' And you said it in a way that sounded like you knew exactly where that was. Please tell me, Eliza. I need to see her."

"Josiah, come here," said Eliza. She reached into her pocket and drew out the 1912 silver coin to show him.

"Eliza! You were there! I was right!"

"Yes, you're right, and you're the only one I can show my prize to! Now tell me why you want to see Jenna."

"Eliza, I made such a bad mistake telling her to leave me alone. I love her. I want to marry her, and I need to tell her that. And," he hesitated, "I'm sorry to tell you this, but I've decided that I can't live without her, so I'm going to move to the future—to her Red Bluff. That's what I want to tell her."

"Jenna will be pleased to hear that, Josiah. Here's how to get there."

Eliza described how to get to Jenna's house in detail, starting with passing the side trail where Josiah and Jenna had caught Hilary Clinton. She described how long it would take him and what to look for once he got close.

"Thanks, Eliza! I'm going right now. Bye," he said as he walked out the door.

A rancher stopped him on the street saying there was another dispute over a cow that Josiah had to handle. Josiah told him that it wouldn't be today and then kept walking toward the livery stable to get Patches. The dog, Bingo, followed at his heels.

As they turned off the main road to the trail that led

to the cave, Josiah turned around to look. This was the place he had called home, the place he loved. He glanced up at the sky and saw white, puffy clouds. There was a chance he would leave this place now and never return. Without a trace of sadness, he exhaled, headed toward the cave, and smiled. He was going to his love. Nothing else mattered.

Josiah had come through the cave and had passed the turnoff where they caught Hilary Clinton, when he saw another rider approaching him. The rider was on a palomino horse. When the horse approached, Josiah recognized the rider. It was Granny!

"Granny! Where are you going all alone?"

"I wasn't aware that someone seventy-five years old required a chaperone, cowboy. Where are *you* going all alone?"

"I'm going to see Jenna, to tell her I love her. And to ask her to marry me."

"It's about time, cowboy! That's all I can say. No, I can say something else. If Jenna says yes, then maybe we can have a double wedding! Edward and I are getting married this weekend!"

Josiah smiled. "I would like nothing better, Granny."

"Do you know how to get to Jenna's ranch?"

"Eliza gave me instructions."

"Okay, good. You're on the right trail. Keep following it, and you will see a pasture and a gate. Go through the gate. And let me give you some advice, cowboy. Go directly into the house. Do not knock on the door. Just walk right in. It will be a better entrance that way."

"What if I'm at the wrong house?"

"Easy. Look in the barn and make sure that Magic is there."

269

"Thanks, Granny!"

"Good luck, cowboy," said Granny as she rode past him toward the cave.

Josiah felt so excited that he could barely sit in the saddle. He was going to see his love and had the blessings of her grandmother. Granny suggested they have a double wedding! Oh, Jenna, Jenna, I love you so much! He wanted to shout it to the world, but instead he rode on until he found the pasture gate that Granny had mentioned. Since Patches had never been through anything like that, Josiah dismounted, led the horse through with Bingo following, and then closed the gate and remounted.

Josiah had a smile on his face a mile wide. When he came to the barn, he looked in and saw Magic there. He had arrived. After putting Patches into the stall across from Magic, he took a deep breath and walked to the front door.

Following Granny's instructions, he put his hand on the door handle, turned it, and walked inside. It was a big house, and Granny had neglected to tell him which way to go once he got inside. But Jet, Jenna's dog, came out to greet Bingo. Josiah walked the way Jet came from.

"Granny? Is that you? Did you forget something?" Jenna asked from the other room. Her voice sounded different, and he heard her sniff.

Josiah walked over and watched as she came to a sitting position and faced him. Tears streaked her face. The sight of her overcame him. He kneeled down next to the couch and said, "Jenna, oh my beautiful Jenna, why are you crying?"

CHAPTER SIXTY-TWO

JENNA, SHOCKED AT the sight of him, cried out, "Josiah!" and raised her arms to hug him. He hugged her so tight that she knew it would be all right—even before he pulled away, looked into her eyes, and said, "Jenna, I love you. I love you so much!"

"I love you, too, Josiah."

"Why are you crying? I wanted to tell you the other night how much I loved you, but you wouldn't talk to me."

"I was afraid you'd tell me not to return to Red Bluff again—like you did before."

Hugging her again, he sat beside her on the couch and said, "I'm sorry I made you afraid. I'm sorry I made you feel bad. I love you so much, Jenna. I've never loved anyone the way I love you."

Before she could answer, he said, "Oh, wait," and knelt on the floor. He got up on one knee, took her hands, and said, "Jenna Leyton, I love you. I want to spend my life with you. Would you do me the honor of being my wife?"

Jenna felt the warmth of his hands, saw the seriousness in his beautiful blue eyes, and started crying again. She had wanted this for so long, and he had pushed her away for so long, that she couldn't believe it was really happening. Trying to catch her breath, she said, "I love you, too, Josiah."

He hugged her again—so tight that she could feel his heart beating against hers. That's when she knew it was real, knew he was finally hers.

Josiah pulled back from the embrace and said, "Jenna, you never answered my question. Oh, before you do, I want to say this. I know it would be difficult for you to give up all the conveniences of modern life, like cars and trucks, so I want you to know that I'm willing to come live in *your* Red Bluff, in *your* time. I don't know what I'll do here, but if you're with me, I don't care. So, with that in mind, I ask again: Will you marry me, Jenna?"

Jenna looked at him and said, "No."

Confused, Josiah tilted his head and said, "No? What do you mean, no?"

"I mean I won't marry you if you intend to live here."

"I don't understand. I thought you wouldn't want to leave here. Oh, because of Granny?"

"How do you know about—oh, you met her on the trail," Jenna said. Josiah nodded. "No, Josiah. I am happy that Granny has moved to the nineteenth century, because that is where I want to live. I'll marry you if we can live there."

Josiah's gaze softened. "You mean it?"

"Do you know who bought Annie's ranch?" Jenna asked. When Josiah shook his head, Jenna answered, "I did!"

"*You* did? You're kidding!"

"No, Josiah, I'm not kidding. I paid for it by cashing in

272

those coins that you gave me! And Ryan is going to fix it up for me with some *modern* conveniences. It was always my plan to live in the nineteenth century. With you. Only with you. Always with you." She kissed him.

"Jenna, I'm so sorry I kept telling you that I never wanted to see you again. It wasn't just that you were from another time. Part of it was that I felt scared. I've never had these feelings before for anyone, and they scared me. Can you ever forgive me?"

"You're already forgiven. How soon were you thinking we should get married?"

"I was thinking, with Granny, this weekend."

"You wouldn't mind?"

"Mind? I think it would be perfect! One thing, though, Jenna."

"Yes?"

"Can you bring more of that cake and ice cream? Maybe the chocolate cream pie? I'm thinking of how much Edward liked it," smiled Josiah.

"For Edward, right," laughed Jenna. "We can arrange that!"

Josiah kissed her softly and looked at her. "And Jenna?"

"Yes?"

"Now show me the wavy thing that Eliza told me about!"

THE END

If you liked this book, sign up on our mailing list to be notified of the next Cowgirls in Time book!

In *Wind Beneath My Wings*, read how Matthew and Sarah struggle with their feelings for each other, until something happens that could tear them apart forever.